# DEATH ROW JOURNAL

Matthew Jared Groce

Copyright © 2008 by Matthew Jared Groce

*Death Row Journal*
by Matthew Jared Groce

Printed in the United States of America

ISBN 978-1-60647-701-4

All rights reserved solely by the author. The author guarantees all contents are original and do not infringe upon the legal rights of any other person or work. No part of this book may be reproduced in any form without the permission of the author. The views expressed in this book are not necessarily those of the publisher.

Unless otherwise indicated, Bible quotations are taken from The New International Version of the Bible. Copyright © 1973, 1978, 1984 by International Bible Society.

www.xulonpress.com

# 1

It was a bright Monday morning in Franklin. I had never appreciated the city's quaint beauty until now, my last week on the job before my next step up the career ladder: Covering the statehouse for the Capital Observer.

Driving through the well-groomed downtown area, I was almost euphoric as I contemplated my next position. I had anticipated the new job for two years. My career path was right on schedule. I would work hard and excel at the Observer, and within three years would be on my way to Washington. I could almost smell the White House briefing room. I would be there to report on — perhaps even expose! — the next big scandal in Washington. I couldn't wait. I relished the prospect of someday being a regular on the McGregor Group or another other prominent talk show. I was confident my writing would one day help fix some of the nation's problems.

I had a light week in store. They hadn't found a replacement for me – confirming my suspicion that I was irreplaceable — but my editor had only planned a couple of assignments for me, freeing me up to take care of packing and other chores. To his credit, he understood my need to move on. In my time there I had elevated the paper's stature, and it was the right time to go.

I was en route to one last visit to City Hall, an unannounced drop-in with the city manager to thank him one final time for his cooperation in my expose on kickbacks in the building department. That piece, as much as anything, had secured me my new job. I had received an Excellence in Investigative Journalism award from the state wire service for the series.

I was in quite a reflective mood. As I pulled up to a red light at Elm and Hopson, my mind flashed back to my first job as a cub reporter at the Plattsville Daily Record. I recalled covering the big annual event: The August visit of the Beeville Women's Mud Wrestling Team. I shuddered.

My trip down memory lane was interrupted when I glanced at my phone and saw there was a message. I muttered that it had once again gone unrung, then smiled as I contemplated yet another perk of my upcoming job — a more reliable phone.

The light turned green just as I called to get the message. It was a woman's voice.

"Mr. Jamison, you are needed at the Lawson Penitentiary as soon as possible. There is a matter of concern on death row. The facility is located 30 miles west of Franklin on County Road 58. Thank you."

Lawson Penitentiary. Why hadn't I ever heard of it? Granted, I had only been in Franklin two years, but prisons were a big deal wherever they were located, and I prided myself on my thoroughness. I reasoned that the 30-mile distance may have kept it off my radar screen.

I glanced at my watch. It was still early, so I had plenty of time to drive out, see what the fuss was about, then come back and stop in at City Hall. I decided to make a return call to the facility to get further information. I checked the incoming calls menu, but for some reason it was not listed. I considered calling the paper to get the number, but didn't want to risk talking to the intrepid Ralph, my fellow reporter.

That was another perk of the new job – no Ralph to deal with. He would want to know all about the call from the prison and perhaps even go with me. Ralph was an amiable fellow, but Franklin was as far as his career would ever take him, and he seemed content with that.

Feeling footloose, I made a couple of turns, passed the community center where I had tutored middle school kids, and headed out 58.

\* \* \* \* \*

As I drove, I began to think further about the message. My mind started racing. What did that mean, "a matter of concern" on death row? Was there a riot? A lump formed in my throat as I pictured serial killers on the loose with skulls-and-crossbones or "Mother" tattooed on their arms.

No, wait, that couldn't be it. They wouldn't bother calling me personally if they were in the midst of a crisis. Would they?

As I headed out 58, I thought for a moment about how, when I was a boy, my alcoholic father had almost wound up in jail after striking my mom. That was the nearest I had ever come to personally encountering the criminal justice system. It was a painful memory, so I quickly pushed it aside.

Following the meandering road, my thoughts returned to a happier subject — my future. Someday I would be able to focus exclusively on my first love, politics, where the real action could be found. I could barely contain my excitement.

One pit stop at Quik Mart for a cup of coffee and a few beads of sweat later, I saw a guard tower looming on the horizon. It was an ominous sight. Fences rose 30 feet off the ground, with a thick cover of tightly wound barbed wire on top. It seemed inescapable.

I parked the Ford, with "The Franklin Mirror" emblazoned on the driver's side door, and slowly emerged from the car. A chill went down my spine. This would be the first time I was to enter a detention facility of any kind. I reminded myself I was a professional reporter and could handle whatever came my way.

I walked up to the gate and pressed a large button. A woman's voice came over the speaker. It was scratchy, much like that of the cashier at a fast-food drive-thru lane. That reminded me: I was getting hungry. My stomach started to growl. I regretted not picking up a muffin with my coffee.

"May I help you?"

"Uh, yes. This is Evan Jamison with the Franklin Mirror."

There was a long pause. I glanced up and saw a surveillance camera pointed directly at me. I felt exposed. I looked down. I noticed a smudge on my left shoe. Finally the voice responded.

"You are granted authorization to enter. The gate will automatically open. You will see a door with a red light above it about 20 yards ahead of you. Proceed to that door and push the button. When you hear the buzz, turn the latch downward and push hard. After you enter, the warden will meet with you."

I heeded the instructions and opened the heavy steel door, only to be confronted by another door five feet later. Again, a buzz, and again I pushed down on the handle and opened the door. Through a glass partition I could see a face and surmised that it was the person with whom I had just been speaking. She gave me a polite half-smile and a slight nod.

I stayed put, waiting for the warden. I thought about the prison movies I had seen in the past. More than one had depicted the warden as corrupt and cruel. I began to wonder if this one would be a good interview.

Then it struck me: There was nothing out of sorts at this prison. In my apprehension, I hadn't noticed the fact that there were no police cars, no ambulances, no helicopters flying overhead, no guards with guns drawn. I heard no rattling of bars, no yelling or screaming. Obviously I had guessed correctly that there was no crisis. So why was I called? Perhaps there was an inmate who had requested time with a reporter. Maybe he wanted to declare his innocence or, conversely, confess to more crimes.

Just then a door swung open. I was startled. I hadn't even seen it. I braced myself. Then came my next surprise. Out into the hall stepped a middle-aged man in his 50s, African-American, with thinning salt-and-pepper hair. He had a slight build and could not have been taller than 5'6". Being just short of six feet myself, I felt positively tall next to him.

But what really caught my attention was his face. It was nothing like what I had expected. As he extended his hand, his eyes locked onto mine, and, so help me, what came to mind was peacefulness. His expression was soft and kind. He did not at all match my preconceived notion of what a warden was supposed to look like.

"Mr. Jamison?"

"Yes."

"Gabriel Paige." He took my hand and shook it firmly. "I am the warden of this facility. I'm pleased that you could come."

"Uh...thank you."

"Won't you come in and have a seat?" He gently put his hand on my back and guided me into his office. I sat down in a straight-back chair facing his desk. The office was clean and tidy but sparsely decorated.

"Would you like something to drink?"

"No...no, thank you." My curiosity was getting the best of me. I looked at the warden, who was maintaining the same kindly expression. "Mr. Paige, do you know why I'm here?"

"Oh, yes."

"Would you mind telling me, please?"

"I didn't mean to alarm you." He must have sensed the concern in my voice.

"Oh, so it was you who directed that I be called?"

"Yes. I must say, the Mirror is a fine paper. I've read many of your articles. They were all very well done."

"Thank you. Now, if you don't mind, I skipped an important appointment this morning to come out here." Okay, so that was a slight exaggeration. "Would you mind telling me what this is all about?"

"By all means. I'm sorry to have left you guessing. I would like to give you the opportunity to interview some of our inmates on death row."

"May I ask why?"

He leaned forward. "I think you'll find their stories of great interest."

I was still a bit nervous but couldn't resist a stab at humor. "Don't tell me...they want to complain about the food."

The warden chuckled. "I believe you will find their complaints run deeper than the quality of their meals."

"Wait a minute. So you actually want to give them a forum?"

"In a sense, yes."

"Why call me?"

"For one thing, you're a good reporter. But there's a more important reason which will become clear later."

I enjoyed the compliment, but that last statement intrigued me. He had my interest. Ordinarily I would have wanted time to prepare some questions, but in this case it seemed there was no time like the present.

"Will you be accompanying me to the cells?"

"I will escort you to each cell, but you will meet with each of them alone so they can speak freely to you, and you to them."

"But no guards?"

He probably could read the apprehension on my face. "I assure you, Mr. Jamison, you will be safe."

I looked him in the eye. I still felt uneasy, but I believed him. There was something about the warden that I could not put my finger on. Whatever it was, he seemed far too kind, too dignified, to run a facility like this.

He continued. "I'm sure you will have some questions to ask of me. I will be happy to talk to you after you have concluded your interviews with the inmates. If you're ready, you can follow me now."

I stood up and suddenly felt lightheaded. I hoped he could not sense the fear welling up inside of me. I was about to stand face to face with hardened criminals waiting to die! *"Try to look professional,"* I reminded myself. I picked up my notebook from his desk and followed him toward the door, hoping I would be leaving this place in one piece.

I had one more question. "Are they expecting me?"

"No, they know nothing about this."

# 2

Paige led me down a hall to the first cell. In my mind I had pictured open-air cells with bars in front, but instead this one was completely enclosed. The cell had a steel door with a small clear plastic window. As he took his keys and prepared to unlock the door for my first interview, he turned and said, "The name of this inmate is Anthony Johnson."

He unlocked the door and motioned me inside. I slowly walked in and heard the door clang shut behind me. Suddenly I felt like the Cowardly Lion.

Johnson had been asleep with his back to me. The slamming of the door had jarred him awake. Up stood a bear of a man. I had never considered myself short...until now. Johnson had at least eight inches on me, but more importantly, a good hundred pounds. He was African-American and appeared to be in his mid 30s.

"Mr. Johnson?" I stammered. "I'm a reporter with the Franklin Mirror. I was asked to come here to interview you."

"What?"

"Believe me, I'm just as confused as you are. But would you mind if I ask you a few questions?"

Johnson raised an eyebrow and looked me over. "You scared, man?"

"A little, yeah."

"A little?"
"Okay...a lot."
Johnson burst into laughter. "Maybe you should be. Maybe you should. But go on and ask me your questions, Mr. Reporter Man. I ain't never been interviewed before."
"Well, I guess my first question is an obvious one. How did you end up on death row?"
He looked me in the eye and smirked. "Murder one."
"I see." I paused, casting a quick glance at the door, wondering whether the warden was ready to get me at a moment's notice. I took a deep breath. "And did you do it?"
"Did I do it?" He again broke into laughter. "Don't you know everybody in here is innocent, man? Nah, I'm just messin' with you. Course I did it. I'd do it again. Only thing I wish is I didn't get caught so I could be takin' care a mo' business on the street."
"Who was your victim?"
"Dude from the 'hood. Owed me 50 for some crack. I warned him he better pay up. Can't have no one skip out. Then everybody think they can skip out on A.J. Ain't no way I can let that happen."
Despite my personal ambivalence toward the death penalty, it was difficult for me to feel sympathy for this man. He was a remorseless killer.
He frowned. "Fool warden says that ain't the only reason I'm here."
"Oh?"
"Says I'm here for sellin' crack to kids."
It took a moment for that to sink in. "Wait. You say you're also on death row for selling drugs?"
"That what he say, man. Told me the judge don't take kindly to that."
"Mr. Johnson, there must be some misunderstanding. I don't condone selling drugs to minors, but that act does

not warrant the death penalty. Murder, yes, but not selling drugs."

"Tell that to the fool warden. Shoot. He throw'd all these names at me an' told me how they ended up 'cause a me."

"Names? You mean the people to whom you sold drugs?"

"That right. Man, I don't even know their names. How he s'pose to know them?"

"That's very interesting." That was an understatement. There was no way the warden could know the names of this man's drug clients. Could he?

I wanted to push the matter further, but with several people still remaining to interview, I decided not to linger. Besides, I felt quite uneasy standing face to face with this man. In any event, it was obvious I would have some questions for the warden.

As I moved toward the door, he added one more thing. "He be sayin' I'm selfish and out for number one. What a fool thing to say. You mean to tell me he ain't? Ain't nobody who ain't selfish!"

Again I wanted to dig deeper, but felt a more pressing need to move on. "Thank you, Mr. Johnson. You've been very helpful."

"Ain't no thang."

I tapped on the door and immediately the warden opened it. Once we were alone in the hall, he gave me the same genial smile and said, "What did you think?"

"Not someone I'd like to meet in a dark alley, if that's what you're getting at."

"Indeed. But did you get any…surprises?"

"As a matter of fact, yes. He told me he faced the death penalty for some lesser offenses."

"He does seem to think so."

"Like selling drugs? Mr. Paige, I'm sure you know distribution is not a capital offense."

"Mr. Jamison, I'll be happy to discuss that matter with you later. Let's proceed to the next interview."

I braced myself, wondering if the next inmate would be as imposing as the first.

\* \* \* \* \*

We moved down the dank hall another 10 feet and arrived at another steel door. The warden quickly unlocked it. This time he ushered me in and lingered for a moment in the doorway.

Sitting on the bed was an Hispanic man in his 20s. He slowly lifted his head and looked in my general direction. An expression of despondency was etched on his face.

"Mr. Jamison, this is Miguel Santos." With those words of introduction, the warden again shut the door behind me.

"Hello, Mr. Santos. My name is Evan Jamison. I'm a reporter with the Franklin Mirror."

He remained silent.

"Mr. Santos, I'd like to ask you just a few questions. Would that be okay?" I noticed a tattoo of a dragon on the side of his neck.

He finally looked at me. "Habla espanol? Do you speak Spanish?" He had a noticeable accent, but still was easily understandable.

"No, I'm sorry, I don't. Just a few words, I'm afraid."

At that moment Santos lowered his head and began to sob.

"Mr. Santos, I didn't mean to upset you."

It took him a couple of minutes to regain his composure enough to respond. "No, sir, I do not cry because of you. I cry because of what I have done. I belong here."

"Well, may I ask why you're here?"

"I stabbed a man."

"I see. And he died?"

"No, he did not die, but he was badly hurt. I heard he is better now."

"Uh, what do you mean?"

"I have a very bad temper. I stabbed him in a fight."

"No, I mean, why are you here on death row? Wounding someone with a knife is not punishable by death."

"You don't understand, sir. That's not what I thought at first either. But I now know it is the right punishment."

"Mr. Santos, first of all, you don't need to call me sir. Second, you may not realize this, but we have a very orderly judicial system. It's not perfect, but it's the best in the world and it is very orderly. There are sentencing guidelines for different crimes, and I can assure you that assault with a deadly weapon is NOT punishable by death."

Santos stood up and slowly took a few steps away from me and faced the wall. He stood motionless for several moments, then turned around. "Sir, the warden has explained that the judge finds my crime deserving of death. Actually, he says it wasn't just the stabbing. He said the stabbing was a symptom."

A symptom? What in the world did that mean? I was thoroughly bewildered and was becoming anxious to get some answers from the kindly Mr. Paige.

"Could you please explain?"

"A symptom of a deeper problem. He told me my temper was an indication I had to have things my way. I now know he is right."

I didn't want him calling me sir anymore, so I tried to get more informal. "Did you say your name is Miguel?"

"Yes, sir." So much for that idea.

"Miguel, I don't think you understand. Trying to have things your own way does not warrant the death penalty!"

He raised his voice. "No, sir, YOU don't understand. It's what I deserve! I am grieving over the troubles my temper has caused. I have hurt many people — not just physically, but emotionally also."

I wanted to explain that there was a difference between guilty feelings and a just sentence, but he had made it clear he didn't want to hear that. Besides, I wanted to talk to the warden right away to make sure he understood a mistake had been made. I thanked Miguel and told him I hoped to see him again. I tapped at the door and the warden opened it immediately.

I looked straight at him. "Did you know that man didn't commit murder? It was assault with a deadly weapon. He's not supposed to be on death row!"

Paige once again gave me a pleasant smile. "Mr. Jamison, I appreciate your concern. But as I said, your questions will have to wait until you have conducted a few more interviews. Please understand."

I was anxious for some answers, but decided to cooperate. I followed him down the hall. "I've got to tell you, Mr. Paige, this is going to make a very interesting story. It'll be a great way to finish my time at the Mirror. By the way, did you know I'll be leaving Franklin soon? I've accepted a position with the Capital Observer."

"Yes, as a matter of fact, I was aware of that. Congratulations."

"So I'm going to want some answers from you before I leave here today."

"That's fine. Just be patient."

I could not understand this man. Why would he invite me to interview someone on death row who clearly didn't belong there? This had the makings of a huge scandal that would very likely cost him his job.

\* \* \* \* \*

We reached the next cell. As the warden put the key in the lock, he paused and said, "This one may have some surprises as well."

He was right. I walked in the door to find a tall blonde woman in her 30s briskly pacing back and forth. Her hair was perfectly coiffed and seemed entirely out of place with her orange prison jumpsuit. But a woman on death row...in a cell right next to a man's?

She stopped and glared at Paige. "Is this an attorney? He'd better be!"

"No, actually, this is a reporter. His name is Evan Jamison and he's from the Franklin Mirror."

"A reporter?" She looked at me and broke into a sardonic smile. "Fine. That's almost as good as a lawyer."

Paige continued his introduction. "Mr. Jamison, this is Elizabeth Kelson." With that, he was out the door again, and the floodgates opened.

"It's a good thing you're here. I can't believe he actually allowed you to see me. Have I got a story for you. You've got to report this. I'm being held against my will! I shouldn't be here. I didn't do anything! I haven't had a trial. I haven't even been formally charged. And he has the nerve to tell me I'm on death row? He is an evil man — an evil man."

She continued, moving her arms demonstrably. "I have never been treated in such an appalling manner in my entire life. How dare they! I know my rights! Haven't they ever heard of due process?"

I was at a loss for words. This whole thing was becoming surreal. The thought finally occurred to me to call the news desk and give them a hint that something big was going on at the Lawson Penitentiary.

"Ms. Kelson, could you please hold that thought for a minute? I have a call to make."

"They let you bring your phone in? Great! Get the word out. Then let me borrow that phone of yours. They haven't even given me my supposed one phone call."

I pulled the phone out of my pocket and looked at the screen. No signal. "It looks like that call will have to wait. I'm sorry, I'm not getting a signal."

"I should have known. Paige probably had something to do with that."

I tried to reassure her. "Actually, I'm sure it's just the walls. I'll call out as soon as I can." Inwardly I suspected the fault lay with the Mirror's cheap phone.

She continued her rant. "This whole thing is an outrage. I am a professional businesswoman. I should not be here at all, much less surrounded by cold-blooded killers!"

Suddenly I thought of Anthony Johnson right down the hall. It was true; she had nothing in common with him. And what in the world was a woman doing on the same cell block with men?

But then a strange thought occurred to me. She actually reminded me of Johnson in some indefinable way. Maybe it was the self-absorption. But then, I reasoned, her attitude was justifiable if what she said was true.

"Ms. Kelson, you say you haven't been formally charged. Have they given you any reason at all for your incarceration?"

She folded her arms, displaying delicately lacquered fingernails. She began muttering to herself.

"I beg your pardon?"

"It's Paige. I blame him for this."

"What has he told you?"

"He claims there's a judge who knows what I did at the bank."

"Bank?"

"Union Trust Bank. It's where I work...or worked, I should say. I'm sure my job is long gone. It's hard to hold a job if you don't show up for work."

"What kind of job?"

"I'm — I *was* an executive at the corporate office. I loved my job. I was good at it. But now it's gone for sure."

"What exactly did the warden accuse you of doing?"

"I'd rather not discuss it."

"Ms. Kelson, in order to give an accurate report, I'll need more details from you. That will help your case."

"I said I'd rather not discuss it," she snapped.

I wasn't going to let her evasiveness off without a fight. "Surely he gave you some reason for being here."

She shot me a brief but intense glance. "He claims that I put my hand in the cookie jar, if you must know."

I paused a minute before continuing. "Forgive my directness...but did you?"

She looked away and stared into space.

"Ms. Kelson?" Still no response.

"Ms. Kelson, did you embezzle money?"

"I told you I don't wish to discuss it! Why don't you ask him? He claims that the bank doesn't even know about it, but that the judge does. Where does he come up with that?"

"But did you do it?"

For a brief moment she looked me in the eye, then looked away just as quickly. There was a long silence. Finally she spoke, abruptly changing the subject.

"You know what really galls me? He also says I'm here because I'm not a good mother." Her voice jumped up two octaves. "Who does he think he is? I love my kids!"

I wanted to calm her, so I tried to focus on her children. "How many kids do you have?"

She again briefly glanced my way. "Two. Two daughters. They're the best kids in the world."

"What are their names?"

"Annie and Erin." Her eyes began to well up.

"How old are they?"

"Nine and seven."

At the risk of setting her off again, I returned to her complaint. "What exactly did he say?"

"He told me I put my career ahead of my kids. Why does he think I work so hard? It's for them!" She began to choke back tears. "He said I put my own needs above theirs. He said my boyfriend shouldn't be living with me. How dare he! Who does he think he is to judge me like that?"

By now she was crying hard and beginning to shake. I was concerned she might break into convulsions. She was in no condition to answer any more questions. I quietly said, "Thank you for your time."

I stood and tapped at the door. She looked up at me and said, through her tears, "Tell the world what has happened to me!"

As the warden opened the door, I thought to myself that she seemed like a perfect candidate for the Jerry Spangler Show. Sadly, she would not be a sympathetic witness in her own defense before a jury if given the chance. But she certainly did not belong here.

I stepped into the hall, stopped and turned to the warden as he closed the door. "Do you mean to tell me that woman is on death row?"

"That is correct."

I shook my head. "Mr. Paige, you seem like a nice man. But I think it only fair to warn you that you probably won't like the article I'm going to write."

"Mr. Jamison, I understand you have some questions and concerns. I assure you, I will be happy to discuss this further at the appropriate time. For now, we have more people for you to interview."

"But that woman didn't even commit a violent crime!"

"Please…later."

I could not understand this man. Still, something compelled me to keep going along with him. I wondered what else lay in store.

*****

The next detainee was a white man with neatly trimmed brown hair. I guessed him to be in his early 40s. His name was Robert McIntosh. He was sitting on his bed, expressionless.

"Mr. McIntosh, I'm a reporter. I'm here to interview you."

He looked up at me. "Is that so? What's your name?" He had a deeply resonant voice.

"Evan Jamison. I work for the Franklin Mirror."

His face brightened. "Hey, I know you! I read your column all the time. It's nice to meet you." He jumped up and extended his hand and shook mine vigorously.

With such an exuberant greeting, for a moment I nearly forgot where I was. I then remembered to focus on the task at hand.

"Mr. McIntosh, I'm sure the warden has given you a reason for your incarceration."

"Yes. Yes, he has." He put his hands on his hips. "I've got to tell you, Evan, I'm none too happy being here. I've got important responsibilities."

"Oh? What do you do for a living?"

"I'm a salesman - a good one. One week last month I brought in 3K in commissions. I really need to get this matter resolved soon."

"What brought you here?"

He broke into a laugh. "Get this — adultery! Can you believe it? I'm surprised Paige didn't sew a scarlet 'A' on my jumpsuit."

I wanted to laugh myself. "Well, sir, I guess I need to ask: Is it true?"

He gave me a bemused look. "Uh...I'm a salesman, remember? I spend a lot of time on the road. I've got a lot of stress in my job. I need a release, and that's how I get it. Then there's Angie, our receptionist. She is hot. Hey, you're a man. You know what I'm talking about."

"So I gather you're married?"

"Oh, yeah — 16 years. Missy's a great lady."

"I take it she doesn't know all this."

"Are you kidding? That would really be death row, you know what I'm saying?" He burst into uproarious laughter.

"Okay, so you are aware this is death row."

"Oh, yeah."

This whole thing was becoming like some kind of theater of the absurd. I tapped my pen on my notepad. "Frankly, Mr. McIntosh, I have no idea why you've been placed on death row, but does it make you at all nervous?"

His tone became serious. "Look, Evan, as I said, I'm not happy being here. This is costing me a lot of money. I know I'm no saint, but it's ridiculous I'm stuck in this place." He ran his hand through his hair.

He got a pensive look on his face. "I know I've got my faults, but overall I'm a really good person. I love my wife. I take good care of her. Besides, I've heard whispers about this judge. I hear he's a good guy. Maybe after he throws out my case, he and I can go have a beer together."

I thanked him for his time. As I waited for Paige to open the door, I thought to myself I had hit the mother lode with this story.

\* \* \* \* \*

On I went, meeting others like McIntosh with seemingly no criminal background: A thirty-something father of two with an Internet gambling addiction; a woman in her 50s who said Paige had accused her of controlling her young adult children; an entrepreneur who had used fraud to reach multimillionaire status; even a man about my age who was obsessively jealous of his successful older brother.

I began to think about my own father and the case against him if he were ever to wind up in this place. I briefly entertained the thought that this was precisely where he belonged.

I had lost all track of time. It felt as if I had been there for hours. There was one last inmate to interview before my much-anticipated conversation with the warden. This was a middle-aged woman of Asian descent named Susan Liu, who appeared to be approaching 60. When I entered the cell, she was sitting quietly on her bed, reading. She seemed more at ease than anyone before her.

"Ms. Liu, thank you for allowing me to speak to you."

"That's fine, young man. I appreciate the company." She put a bookmark in her book and laid it on the pillow, then adjusted her jumpsuit.

"May I ask what you are doing here, ma'am?"

"You certainly may. This is one of those cases of mistaken identity. I'm not supposed to be here." She laughed softly. "I never thought this kind of thing would happen to me. But I'm not worried. I'm sure they will figure that out soon and release me."

I pressed on. "Well, rest assured, I'm not here to accuse you of anything. But could you please tell me what reason the warden gave for your arrest?

"It's not even worth discussing. As I told you, I think they have me mixed up with someone else."

I decided to tread carefully, but was determined to get something out of her. "Well, just out of curiosity, what did they wrongly charge you with?"

"Oh, it's rather silly. They say I haven't been active in helping others. They say I spend too much time watching soap operas and reading romance novels. Well, that's just plain wrong. I am a very religious person. Personally, I don't see anything wrong with books and TV, but it's not like I'm addicted to them."

"Ma'am, you do understand you're on death row, don't you? That means you're scheduled for execution unless you get out of this."

"Oh, I'm not worried. Of course I want to go home, but I'm content with my reading until they sort things out."

I glanced down and saw a paperback with a drawing of a scantily clad couple on the cover.

"Well, ma'am, I'm going to be speaking to the warden, so hopefully that will help get this resolved."

She smiled and said, "Anything you can do to help, I would certainly appreciate."

"I'll do what I can. Thank you again for your time."

As Paige opened the door for me, I wondered how this woman could remain so serene.

And now, at long last, I would have my opportunity to speak to the person responsible for all this. I had tried to be patient, but now I was anxious to get some answers. I was appalled that these people were stuck in this place – except for the first one. He belonged here. But the rest? Not a chance.

This escapade served to remind me how much I appreciated my chosen profession. I was regularly exposed to dysfunctional people – in my mind, every one of these "inmates" fit that category – but as a journalist, I was able to stay detached. My job was to observe and report, not to become emotionally involved. I could stay above the fray and not get sucked into people's idiosyncrasies. Oftentimes I would walk away from my assignments thinking I was the only rational person in the entire state. That was certainly the case today.

This experience would serve me well in my new post. I was all the more eager to head to the capital. But first things first — it was time to go on the offensive against the wiry prison warden.

## 3

Paige escorted me down the hall. "Well, Mr. Jamison, I assured you I would answer your questions. Here's an empty cell where we can talk."

He ushered me in and left the door open. It was identical in its starkness to the other cells – a cot, chair, sink and toilet. He offered me the chair. I declined, choosing to remain standing. Paige opted to do so as well, leaning his back against the wall. He gave me a quick nod and said, "Okay, fire away."

"Well, first, Mr. Paige, I want to thank you for calling me out here today. This is quite a way for me to end my time in Franklin. It's been a very enlightening experience."

"You're welcome."

"I have a lot of questions, but it really comes down to this: How did you do it? How did you manage to get a bunch of people locked up on death row, people that you and I both know don't belong here? As far as I can tell, many of them didn't even commit a crime! Most of them are just guilty of bad choices." A steely determination was welling up inside me to have this place shut down.

Paige looked at me with the same genial expression he had carried all day. "Mr. Jamison, you are correct in one sense. Only one of the people you interviewed committed a crime punishable by death according to federal or state statutes. But there are other laws besides those."

"Other laws? What other laws?"

"Let me answer that with some questions of my own. Is murder wrong? Is assault wrong? Is stealing wrong?"

That was easy. "Yes, of course." What was he getting at?

"And why are they wrong?"

"Why? They're wrong because they're wrong. And there are laws against them."

Paige again smiled. At this point that smile was frankly beginning to offend me.

"Mr. Jamison, you're an intelligent young man. Who's to say assault is wrong? What if I think it's okay to assault someone?"

Inwardly I chuckled trying to picture this small man assaulting anyone. Outwardly I was ready with a reply. "Assault hurts someone. It's wrong to hurt people."

Paige's eyes lit up. "I couldn't agree more! It is wrong to deliberately hurt someone. But may I conclude you think an act is okay if no one is hurt?"

"Sure. Why not?"

"Well, have you ever considered the notion that everything a person does affects others?"

"How so?"

He paused. "Tell me, what did you think of Ms. Liu?"

"The last woman I interviewed?"

"That's the one."

"Well, I'm not sure she was all there, if you know what I mean. I think she was in denial."

"In your discussion with her, did she give any indication that she had hurt someone?"

"I'm glad you asked. The answer is no. She told me the reason she was given for being here was because she watched

TV and read harlequin romances. I suppose you think that justifies her facing the death penalty."

"Well, what Ms. Liu failed to mention is that her next-door neighbor is a shut-in with no family support."

"Your point?"

"Did Ms. Liu do something to hurt someone? No. It's what she didn't do that hurt someone. Perhaps you've heard it said that there are crimes of commission and crimes of omission."

"What crime? Look, I'm sorry her neighbor is lonely. But since when is it a crime to be a bad neighbor?"

"Well, sadly, her neighbor had a stroke last year."

"Oh, and she was supposed to have somehow known and raced to the rescue? Come on, the woman can't see through walls."

"I'll grant you that. But she went for a walk past the neighbor's house every morning and saw the newspapers piling up in the driveway."

"Look, Mr. Paige, I'm not defending the woman. Maybe she could have been a better neighbor. But the fact remains that being a bad neighbor isn't a crime, and especially not a crime punishable by death!" I was thoroughly agitated, but resisted the temptation to let out a cry of frustration.

He then reiterated the same strange point he had made a moment before. "As I said, there are other laws besides those in the U.S. Code or state statutes."

"You still haven't explained that one."

"Well, for now, let me repeat this point: Virtually everything a person does – or doesn't do – affects others and thus has moral implications." Paige then took a couple of quick steps toward the door and said, "I'll tell you what, Mr. Jamison. Why don't you spend some time looking over your notes? I'll be back shortly."

"No, that's okay. I can do that at my office. I have many more questions for you and I'd like to get to them."

"I understand. But please, for now, just make yourself comfortable."

In a flash, he was out the door. It slammed shut.

\* \* \* \* \*

Something was not right. I scurried to the door. It was locked! I feared what that might mean. Was I now incarcerated just like those other people? Impossible! But why else would he leave me locked in here? The thought of it was more than I could bear. I flew into a rage, yelling through the thick steel door. "What's going on here, Paige? Is this some kind of joke? Come back here and let me out. I mean it! Open this door...now!!!" I spewed every profanity imaginable.

I started pounding on the door, to no avail. I would have thrown the chair, but it was bolted to the floor. I resumed my screaming. "I'm a journalist, remember? I'm not supposed to be part of the story! You're making a huge mistake!"

There was no response. I looked out the tiny window and saw nothing. I put my ear to the door. I heard no footsteps, no dangling of keys. I was suddenly and quite unexpectedly alone. In an instant my anger turned to fear verging on panic. This man had already successfully kept many innocent people locked up against their will. Was I now one of them? It couldn't be! What about my new job? Just days from that big step, I found myself locked in a prison cell with no way out. I was no longer in control. I began to scream once again.

"Paige! Let me out of here! LET ME OUT OF HERE NOW!!!" Again, no response.

After a while I finally managed to calm myself, concluding that panicking would do me no good. I began to pace back and forth. Then, finally, after perhaps an hour, Paige turned the key and re-entered the cell. If I had been expecting that,

I would have been ready to run. But he quickly closed the door, preventing my escape.

I glared at him. "You've got a lot of nerve, Paige. Why did you lock me in here? That's it. I need to leave...NOW."

"I'm afraid that's not possible, Evan."

"What do you mean, not possible? This is a free country. Let me out of here!"

At that moment he did something that crossed the line: He gave me that same gentle smile. It was more than I could bear. I had never engaged in physical violence in my entire life, yet I found myself clenching my fist, poised to strike him full force in the jaw. I raised my arm and prepared to swing, but then something happened I never could have expected. My fist stopped in midair. Was it some unseen force, or just my own will convincing me to pull back? Whatever it was, Paige never even flinched.

He looked at me without the smile, but with what seemed like an expression of concern – not for himself, but for me. "Evan, violence will not change your situation."

I felt the blood rush to my head. I finally decided to take the seat he had offered earlier.

It took a couple of moments for me to gather my wits. After taking a deep breath, I felt composed enough to ask another question.

"Mr. Paige, what is going on here? Why are you detaining me?"

"It's very simple. You belong here."

"I belong here? What are you talking about? I'm a neutral observer!" Then I remembered the people I had interviewed. Some of them were here for the most ridiculous of reasons. Of what horrible crime was he going to accuse me? Speeding? Jaywalking?

"Evan, you seem to have a healthy sense of justice."

"As a matter of fact, I do. That's one of the reasons I wanted to be a journalist. I like exposing injustice. And believe me, I've found a great example of it right here!"

"You may think so. But what you don't realize is that the judge also has a strong sense of justice...much stronger than yours, in fact."

I had forgotten about the judge. Several of the people had made vague references to him. "Who exactly is this judge, Paige?" I demanded.

"Well, let me put it this way. I can absolutely, without any equivocation, assure you that he always makes right judgments."

"If he had anything to do with me being locked in this cell, I must emphatically disagree with that statement!" I began to mutter to myself. I had never been more livid. I was too upset to remain seated, so I stood and began once again to pace.

Paige then asked me a question that seemed totally off-topic. "Evan, have you ever read 'Pride and Prejudice'?"

I was incredulous. How could he bring up a work of fiction at a time like this? "What, you mean the novel?"

"Yes."

"Yeah, I read that in my freshman English class in college. What does that have to do with anything?"

"That was a well-written book, don't you think?"

"Yeah, I suppose. But what's your point? What does 'Pride and Prejudice' have to do with this situation?" It was becoming a great challenge to control my emotions.

"As you may recall, that was a story about first impressions and wrong conclusions, particularly by the young woman, Elizabeth Bennet. She misjudged Mr. Darcy. He turned out to be quite different than she first thought... different in a very good way. Some of her conclusions were reasonably drawn based on her own observations, but they turned out to be incorrect. As you may recall, in the end she happily married him."

"For you to detain me shows you've made some wrong conclusions of your own — or that judge friend of yours has."

"Well, actually, my point is not that the judge draws wrong conclusions about people but that people draw wrong conclusions about the judge. I dare say he's more misunderstood than anyone in the world." He looked intently at me, then paused before speaking, as if wanting to make sure I wouldn't miss what he was about to say. "Evan, it was he who made the decision to have you called here."

I felt as if I had been hit over the head. I stopped pacing and turned toward him. "What? You're telling me some nameless judge I've never met abused his authority and tricked me into coming here to have me locked up?"

"As I said, he is frequently the object of mistaken conclusions."

"Listen, Paige, maybe this is some kind of game to you, but I have no interest in playing. You need to let me go."

He stepped toward me. "I assure you, I understand this is no game. Indeed, it is deadly serious. You have broken many laws, and that is no light matter."

Before I could respond to his ridiculous assertion, he raised another unexpected topic. "Evan, let me ask you something. As I said, you're an intelligent young man. Why did you find it necessary to embellish your achievements on your college application?" If nothing else, he seemed intent on throwing curveballs at me.

"Uh...I beg your pardon?"

"You stretched the truth on your college application."

"What? Where did you come up with that?"

"Think back. You gave the impression you were deeply involved in your high school service club when, in fact, you attended meetings sporadically and never once participated in an actual service project."

I had forgotten all about my college application process. How could he possibly know that? "How do you know I was in a service club, anyway?"

"How do you think I know? It's not that I'm a good guesser."

I stared at him, waiting for an answer. "It was the judge, Evan. It was he who told me."

\* \* \* \* \*

How in the world did this so-called judge know about my high school service club? I began to feel a sense of paranoia. Maybe this "judge" was actually some kind of CIA operative and Paige was his contact. Or perhaps someone didn't like my columns and had instigated some sort of dirty tricks campaign such as found on the political campaign trail. But would someone really make the effort to call my high school, get the name of the club's faculty advisor from eight years ago and interview her about me? And, if so, why? This was all beyond comprehension. But how else to explain it? Then I began to think about the banker's statement that the judge had allegedly known about her shenanigans at the office…if indeed that was true.

Paige sat quietly for a moment, apparently wanting to allow his last comment to sink in. He then launched onto yet another topic.

"Evan, I really liked your expose on the kickbacks for those city officials."

Why was he bringing that up? I was skeptical of the compliment. "But?"

"But nothing. It was excellent."

"If I weren't locked in here, I suppose I would say thank-you."

"It was well done. What those officials did was wrong. In part because of your efforts, they were caught."

If he was trying to somehow butter me up, it wasn't working. But then he brought it back around to the accusation. "Tell me something, Evan. What's the difference between cheating by public officials and your cheating on a college application?"

"You're not serious, are you? For one thing, I didn't cheat. But more importantly, they betrayed the public trust and I did not!"

"You attended Relman College, correct?"

"You seem to know everything else about me, so obviously you know the answer is yes."

"They have an excellent journalism program, do they not?"

"Yeah, one of the best." I began to tap my foot impatiently.

"I know it's quite an accomplishment getting accepted there."

I realized where this was going and started to shake my head in disgust.

He continued. "It occurs to me you might have given yourself an unfair advantage over some worthy students by stretching the truth."

I was growing weary of this prosecution and was anxious to change the subject. I decided to excuse my way out of it. "That was several years ago, Paige. I don't remember it very well. But I suppose it's possible I may have exaggerated a little. You know the old saying, 'Nobody's perfect.'"

Paige was ready for that one. "If I had a nickel for every time I've heard that, I'd be quite wealthy." His expression then turned serious and he looked me in the eye. "It's interesting that people say, 'Nobody's perfect' when excusing their own actions, but they are much slower to use that phrase when spotting the faults of others."

I thought that over for a moment. The man had a point. But I wasn't about to admit that to him. I was determined to steer the conversation back where I wanted it. "So, Paige, you're saying that my allegedly spruced-up college application, written when I was all of 18 years old, has me on death row."

Paige replied, "As I said, I merely mentioned it as an example of why you were brought here."

"Oh, so there's more."

"Indeed."

I couldn't resist plunging ahead, if for no other reason than to show the absurdity of it all. "Do tell, then."

"Well, I don't intend to present some kind of laundry list of your shortcomings, Evan."

"Oh, please do. I can take it! Besides, I apparently have all the time in the world." I got up to stretch my legs. I looked over at Paige. "Well? Go ahead. I'm all ears."

"Evan, your college application was just a symptom of a deeper issue."

*Symptom.* One of the inmates had told me Paige used that word with him. Who was it? Ah, yes — Miguel, the young man whose anger was a "symptom."

I smirked. "And what might that 'deeper issue' be?"

"Evan, you have a drive, a determination to make a difference in the world. But a good part of that ambition is motivated by a desire to have others think well of you, to hang on your opinions and laud you in the public square. That's part of the reason you want to keep moving up to bigger and better newspapers. Put in the simplest terms, you're self-centered."

That accusation stung deeply. It was offensive to me on many levels. Who did this man think he was? "Listen, Paige, there's not a thing wrong with wanting a good reputation. You make that sound like a bad thing, as if I'm some selfish boor who's looking out for number one. That is totally wrong. I'm sure you already know this, but I spend some of my limited free time tutoring underprivileged kids. As a matter of fact" — the thought came to me at that very moment — "even if I wasn't very involved in my high school service club, I'd say what I've done as a volunteer in Franklin more than makes up for it."

I was proud of myself for thinking up such a powerful rebuttal to his accusation and hoped that might finally silence him and convince him to let me go. Paige looked at the floor. I thought I finally had him hoisted by his own petard. Then he shook his head slightly, looked up at me and said, "Actually, Evan, that proves my point."

"What are you talking about?"

"Volunteering with kids is a wonderful thing. But I think you will agree with me that your motives weren't altogether altruistic."

The anger was beginning to boil up in me once again, while concurrently my opinion of Paige was sinking lower and lower with each passing moment. His observation about "Pride and Prejudice" had been apt, because it was clear I had gotten the wrong first impression about *him*. I now was convinced he was the most arrogant man I had ever met. How could he question my actions, even my motives? "You can't have it both ways, Paige. You criticized that Liu woman for not looking out for her neighbor, and now you criticize me for helping kids."

"Evan, please understand, I am not criticizing the fact that you tutored. I tried to make that clear. But let's face it. You had selfish motives. You did it in part to cause others to think highly of you so as to enhance your journalistic credentials in the community, in part to project a caring, well-rounded image for your next employer, and in part, if you are brutally honest, to help convince yourself you're a good person."

I cackled at that last zinger. "Paige, I don't need to convince myself I'm a good person! Give me a break, will you?"

But he persisted. "Tell me something. What, in your mind, makes someone a good person?"

"That's easy. A good person is someone who tries to make the world a better place, who doesn't deliberately hurt others, who is true to himself."

It occurred to me that it was time to turn the tables. I wasn't the only one whose definition of goodness could be challenged. Why should I be the only one facing an inquisition? As a matter of fact, wasn't I supposed to be the one asking the questions?

"How about you, Paige? Do you consider yourself a good person?" Finally, a chance to make him squirm. But his answer surprised me.

"Let me put it this way. I'm not my own source of goodness."

"Oh? And what might that mean?" I wasn't sure where this was leading, but felt compelled to take the bait. "Just what is your 'source of goodness'?"

"The judge is my source of goodness."

He was now reaching new heights of folly. I couldn't leave that remark untouched. "Well, of course. You guys really are tight, aren't you?"

"You might say that."

"You're so close that his goodness kind of rubs off on you, huh?" I could not resist the biting sarcasm.

Paige once again had a ready reply. "There's something you need to understand about the judge, Evan. When it comes to goodness, he is the standard-bearer."

"Oh, the standard-bearer! I must say, you seem to hold this guy in very high regard."

"The highest. His laws reflect the goodness of his character."

\* \* \* \* \*

By this time I was beginning to feel quite drained – physically, mentally and emotionally — so it took me a moment to process what Paige had just said.

"Would you mind repeating that?"

"I said his laws reflect the goodness of his character."

"That's what I thought you said. What do you mean, his laws? I thought you said this guy is the judge."

"That's right. He's the judge, and he's also the lawgiver. In fact, it is his laws you have broken."

I was floored. "Paige, are you out of your mind? Haven't you ever heard of separation of powers?"

"Of course. It's one of the greatest strengths of this country."

"Yet you don't see a problem with this guy being both lawmaker and judge?"

Evan, do you understand why the Founding Fathers devised separation of powers?"

"Sure...because they knew what absolute power does. It corrupts absolutely. They had been its victims at the hands of King George."

"Precisely. They knew that human nature is flawed and must be restrained. Thus they devised checks and balances."

I extended my arms in front of me. "Okay, let me get this straight. You do think separation of powers is a good thing, just not in the case of your judge friend." Now I was beginning to see things more clearly. Some lunatic had asserted dominion over his own little world, and Paige was his stooge. "Don't you see, Paige? Your friend is claiming absolute authority, the very thing our nation's laws protect against!"

"Evan, you have a very limited perspective. Remember what I said about the judge being misunderstood? Understand this: Unlike many governmental leaders, he's not corrupt. In fact, unlike any president or king, he is incorruptible. He doesn't need someone else to provide checks and balances for him. He is able to handle both roles, lawgiver and judge, simultaneously."

Paige just didn't get it. He was completely duped by this guy. How could I argue with that? But then I remembered a salient and troubling fact: This lawgiver, judge, whoever he was, somehow knew things about me that he had no discernible way of knowing. That quelled the zeal of my prosecution.

Paige then took a new tack. "Evan, I'm sure it seems, from your perspective, that I'm being tough on you, perhaps even that I've been impugning your character."

I could not resist a sarcastic retort. "No!"

"The fact is, I know you have a desire for this world to be a better place. In fact, I believe you have a stronger sense of right and wrong than most people." He took a slight step closer to me. "But the one you need to compare your goodness to is not your neighbors and co-workers. It's the standard-bearer for goodness — the judge."

I shook my head. "So you're telling me I need to compare myself with someone I've never met who likes making up his own rules. Listen, forcibly holding someone against his will doesn't comport with any reasonable person's understanding of goodness."

Again I welled with pride for managing to continue finding ways to come up with sharp rebuttals under such trying circumstances, but by this time I was beginning to feel spent. Paige must have felt the same, as he sat quietly for several minutes. Maybe at last I had gotten through to him.

Finally he walked over and looked me in the eye. "Evan, remember what I said. The judge is misunderstood. He claims absolute authority, that's true. But he's no Hitler or Stalin. In fact, he's quite the opposite. He's not interested in controlling others for the sake of ego. He's interested in guiding others for their own benefit and for the benefit of those around them."

I wanted to blurt out another slice of sarcasm, but his last statement piqued my curiosity. I decided to let him continue unchallenged.

"His moral laws are rooted in virtue, not domination. You're not the only one who sees that the world is amiss. The reason he hates the breaking of his laws is because he knows how utterly damaged humanity is, and he knows what the world would be like if people did things his way."

As upset as I was, something about that struck a chord in me. While I was far from ready to accept his characterization of the judge, the idealist in me wanted to believe there was someone, somewhere, who was truly virtuous. I knew there were politicians in my own lifetime whom I had at one time idolized, only to see them fall flat. I was now listening intently.

"Evan, the world's ills are built on a foundation of seemingly minor indiscretions."

\* \* \* \* \*

A sobering thought struck me: *Minor indiscretions...like exaggerated college applications.* For the first time, that allegation truly pricked my conscience. As I thought back to my application to Relman, I had indeed been less than honest. I had wanted to go there so badly that I had stretched the truth in an area I thought would impress them – community service.

Then something happened. My thoughts started to broaden to other areas. Somehow a troubling notion began to slip through the defenses of my mind — that I routinely played fast and loose with the truth when it suited me. Perhaps I wasn't as virtuous as I had always assumed.

I did not like where this was going. In no time I had gone from a feeling of resentment to a sense of shame — something I hadn't felt since I was a child. Somehow, something he said had magnified the issue of my truthfulness, or lack thereof, and it was quickly beginning to weigh heavily on me. However, Paige apparently didn't pick up on it, because he proceeded to divert the conversation to a completely unexpected topic.

# 4

"Evan, I need to raise a painful subject with you – your cousin."

My throat tightened. "My cousin Tom?"

"Yes."

I would have welcomed having the focus switched to someone other than me – anyone but Tom. Tom was one of the main reasons I had taken the job with the Mirror in the first place. He had been living in Franklin for a couple of years and had begged me to move there. In my first year at the paper, most of my free time was spent with Tom. But then one night he had lost control of his car and died in a one-car accident. Now, one year later, I was still mourning his loss. How the warden knew anything about Tom spooked me, but if he was about to say something critical of him, I would not be responsible for my actions.

"Please hear me out, Evan. I know how close you were to Tom, and I understand why you loved him so much. He was a vivacious young man. I'm very sorry for your loss."

I was taken aback by the sincerity of his expression of sympathy.

"There's something you don't know about Tom's accident."

I felt the hair on the back of my neck start to tingle. I didn't know how he knew more than I did, but I desperately needed to know what it was.

"Tom did nothing wrong that night. He wasn't under the influence. He didn't fall asleep at the wheel. He wasn't even speeding." He paused.

My heart was racing. "Look, I don't know how you know this, but tell me what happened!"

"He was driving along, heading home, minding his own business, when someone came along from the opposite direction. The driver veered into his lane. Tom swerved to avoid a head-on collision and lost control. That's how he hit that tree."

I stood in stunned silence. The accident was not Tom's fault! I had assumed he had fallen asleep or simply wasn't paying attention to the road. In one sense it was comforting knowing he wasn't to blame. But in a way, this was far worse.

"There's more, Evan."

In my numbness, it took a moment to respond. "What?"

"The reason the other driver was driving erratically was because he was high on drugs. And the person who sold him the drugs that night was someone you've met…Anthony Johnson."

It couldn't be. "Not the first man I interviewed here!"

"The same. I thought you needed to know."

My legs felt weak. I stumbled to the empty chair. Between my mental and physical exhaustion and this shocking news, I could no longer maintain my composure. I broke down and began to cry uncontrollably.

After a while, in the midst of my sobs, I felt Paige's hand on my shoulder. As angry as I had been at him only minutes earlier, I found the gesture strangely comforting.

As my tears finally subsided, Paige quietly said, "Evan, it's late. I'm going to step outside for a little while and let you get some rest. Tap on the door if you need anything."

By this time I was too tired to argue. I desperately wanted to go home, but I welcomed the chance simply to be alone with my thoughts.

\* \* \* \* \*

The news about Tom was devastating. I had only recently begun to come to grips with his death, but Paige's words, while appreciated, had ripped open all the old wounds. Only now it was worse. To think his death was indirectly caused by a man I had met that very day...one who was at that moment right down the hall! I seethed as I thought about that cocky drug dealer and the havoc he had wreaked on our family. I now felt bitterness bordering on rage and wanted to hurt Johnson for what he had done.

How could this have happened? Tom was young, smart, and, as Paige accurately described him, full of life. His death had robbed me of not just my cousin but also my best friend. What kind of world was this where a sleazy character like Anthony Johnson could have determined Tom's fate? And what had compelled some user to get behind the wheel high on drugs?

In my job I had been exposed to the darker side of human nature, but as a journalist I had always been able to keep a professional distance. This, however, was personal. My cousin was gone forever, and two people had selfishly contributed to his death. I started to understand and appreciate why this lawgiver/judge figure would have such a strong reaction to crimes like this.

To make matters worse, I began to confront a painful aspect of Tom's passing. When he died, we had been in the midst of a disagreement. It wasn't our first. I had always reasoned that we were just too much alike…and also that he happened to be in the wrong every time. But I had been filled with regret that things weren't harmonious between us at the time of his death.

Again the tears flowed. Why had this happened? The pain seemed unbearable. I went through another crying jag for several minutes. As it subsided, I felt anxious to put the whole matter on my mind's back shelf for a while so the hurt could abate. I rose from the hard metal chair and started once again to pace. Unfortunately, the only other thoughts that came to mind were the equally disturbing words the warden had uttered about me. I decided it was time to evaluate them. While I had taken offense at his accusations, I also had been trained to pursue the truth in every story I covered, and it was time to weigh his words to see how much they comported with reality.

Had I really cheated on my college application? As I had already begun to admit to myself, yes, I had. It had been easy to rationalize it at the time as a case of the ends justifying the means, but the bottom line was that I had, in fact, lied. Even now I reasoned that I was a better journalist than anyone whose slot I might have taken, but the sobering truth was that what I did was wrong.

What about how he questioned my motives and accused me of selfishness? I bristled at the thought of it. That one had been a low blow. The fact was that I had spent considerable time tutoring kids. I hadn't particularly enjoyed it – they weren't very attentive, they didn't do their homework, and they didn't seem to like me very much – but I had done it nonetheless. So who was he to call me self-centered?

Paige kept saying this judge fellow was misunderstood. How could I misunderstand him if I had no idea who he was? Before today, I had had no preconceived notions of him whatsoever. If he really was the one ultimately responsible for my being locked up here, I was none too happy with him. But still, something intrigued me. Paige said the judge had a great sense of justice. When I thought about Anthony Johnson, I was glad of it. But what about the others I had interviewed? Did they deserve the same fate?

One thing I could acknowledge: Every one of them had something in common with Johnson. They had all been self-obsessed, and every one of them had justified his or her actions – everyone except the strange young man named Miguel. According to his own words, he too had been that way at one time. But as of today he was far from it. Indeed, I had never seen anyone filled with so much remorse.

Then I took another look at myself and the dark thoughts returned. Was I like Miguel? Hardly. What about the others? Was I, like them, one who justified my own wrong actions? Was I really any different than all those other people? Inwardly I gasped at the thought.

Paige had given me what I regarded as a high compliment, one with which I agreed. I was something of an idealist. I wanted the world to be a better place and held out hope it could someday become so. But then I started thinking again about the political leaders I had observed in my own lifetime as well as the ones I knew from history. Every one of them was flawed – even the ones I liked. Oh, they had important roles to play, and they certainly could make a difference at the margins, but they couldn't change the world in a fundamental way because ultimately they were powerless to change human hearts.

All my life, especially since I started working as a journalist, I had lamented the human condition and wanted it to change. Why was there so much hatred and war and poverty in the world? Why were young boys in Africa forced to take up arms and commit atrocities? Why was human trafficking thriving? Why was child pornography rampant? Why were couples in America, who seemed to have it all, getting divorced at an alarming rate? And why did so many people content themselves with drugs and alcohol?

I desperately wanted the world to be a better place, but in this stark cell I was beginning to realize that I too was powerless to really change it. I worked in a worthy profession that effectively exposed injustice, but that alone was not enough to truly change things. It dawned on me that spouting my opinions on the McGregor Group would improve nothing but my own ego. In my profession I spent a lot of time observing people's foibles and character liabilities, but now I was beginning to come face to face with my own. I could not expect everyone else to change without changing myself.

But how? As excruciating as it was to admit, what Paige said was true. Even the good I did was tainted by impure motives. Was it really possible to put aside my own desires for the sake of others?

Then I considered the thorniest proposition of all, one so ghastly I wished I could expel it from my mind. Perhaps I wasn't all that different even from Anthony Johnson. Oh, there was a vast chasm between us in background and in actions, but it was a difference not of kind, but of degree. I had the potential to be just as self-serving as he was.

The despondency I had felt over learning the details of Tom's death was now matched by the sobering reality of my own flawed nature. In my despair I wondered if perhaps I did belong here after all. Earlier I had wanted to meet the judge so I could give him a piece of my mind. But now, taking the time to examine my own heart had given me an instinctive sense that this man truly was good – far better than I. For that reason I somehow felt drawn to see him. Conversely, part of me wanted to be nowhere near him for the simple reason that he had demonstrated, through Paige, that he knew the darkest parts of me, and I felt quite uneasy at the prospect of being face to face with him.

* * * * *

Suddenly I was jolted from my thoughts by the sound of the door opening. Paige was back.

"Hello again, Evan. Were you able to get some rest?"

"My mind's been racing too much for that, I'm afraid."

"Yes, you've had a lot to chew on. I know it was very difficult for you to have to receive the news about your cousin."

"I won't deny that. It was very painful to hear. But actually I'm relieved you told me, and I appreciate it."

"Evan, now that you've had some time to digest that difficult information, there's one other thing I wanted to mention about your cousin."

I shuddered to think there could be more. "Go ahead."

"The judge informed me that while you and Tom were close, you didn't always get along."

Here we went again. Once more he was demonstrating that this judge seemed to know everything about me. I wanted to know how, but every time some new revelation came up, I was too overwhelmed to contest it.

He continued. "I know that even the closest of friends and relatives can argue. I'm not trying to pick on you regarding such a painful subject, but it will help me make a deeper point. Don't you think it's interesting that even the best of friends don't always get along? You and Tom were extremely close, and yet you would still get angry at each other. And each time, both of you thought the other was completely at fault. The truth is that at times both of you acted selfishly toward one another — toward someone you cared for deeply. In fact, Tom was probably the only person you felt was at your level, yet even he, from your perspective, fell short at times. So, you see, you and Tom were just like everyone else. Every human relationship is flawed and has the potential to break down. The main thing people have in common is that, when they're involved in a conflict, they blame the other party and fail to acknowledge their own faults. It's another example of how people are, by nature, basically self-centered."

Paige did not give me much time to contemplate that proposition before hitting me with something else. "Evan, you probably now realize that the judge knows everything about you. He sees that your life has been filled with pride. You've thought you were above everyone else's shortcomings, including at times even people you love. But in fact you are just like everyone else." Perhaps he didn't realize that I had already been beating myself up and no longer needed his assistance in doing so.

Then, unexpectedly, he seemed to pull back on the reins a bit. "But Evan, you need to understand something. I'm not singling you out. Every person you interviewed today has felt wronged. Every one of them has felt unjustly accused."

At that point I felt compelled to come to the defense of the second person I interviewed. "That's not completely accurate. One of them was plagued with guilt."

"You must mean Miguel. Yes, but you didn't see him when he arrived here. You might have a hard time imagining this, but he was an extremely angry young man – probably the angriest person we've had here. But over time, he began to see himself through the judge's eyes, and he didn't like what he saw. None of the others you spoke with has gotten to that point yet. They refuse to see the truth and to acknowledge what a serious thing it is to violate the moral dictates of the Lawgiver – and, in addition, that they are answerable to him. Miguel is miserable right now, but he's reached a milestone. He's begun to face up to his own nature. That's an important first step." I was curious – first step toward what? – but was too drained to ask.

Paige then looked at me and paused. I wasn't sure whether he was hesitant to ask me the next question or if he just wanted to give me time to process what he had been saying. But his query struck me as an odd one. "Evan, what is your opinion of presidential pardons?"

"Could you repeat that?"

"Presidential pardons. What do you think of them?"

"Presidential pardons. Hmm. Well, from what I've seen, I don't care for them." What was he getting at?

"And why don't you care for them?"

"From where I sit, they're undeserved and unjust. It's usually presidents abusing their authority and letting off their cronies who have committed crimes. They get off scot-free."

Paige smiled. "You do have a keen sense of justice, don't you? Now, Evan, I want you to listen carefully to two things. One, you still may not understand this, but you really do belong here. This is not a state facility. It is run by the lawgiver. You have rejected his rightful authority over your life, just as everyone else has...from corrupt government officials to traveling salesmen to drug dealers. You have been a law unto yourself. You have willfully broken his laws. On the surface you are a very good person, but he sees not just your actions but your motivations. He knows your thoughts. He knows how far short you fall from his standards."

I had been looking down, hoping that might somehow diminish the sting of the accusations that were flying at me. But then Paige walked up to me and put his hands on my shoulders. As I held my head up, he looked me directly in the eye. His expression brightened. "Evan, I also have good news for you. It's wonderful news. The judge is willing to grant you a pardon. You don't deserve it any more than a presidential associate does, but it's true. In fact, he's not just willing; he *wants* to pardon you! But that's not all. Listen carefully to what I'm about to say. He doesn't want to just set you free. He wants a *relationship* with you. He wants to be a father to you! In fact, there are others who have spent time at this facility who have been released…and he has legally adopted them."

\* \* \* \* \*

*He wants to be a father to you.* That impacted me even more than his words about pardon. Since this judge already seemed to know everything else about me, it stood to reason that he knew about my own father as well.

I had not seen him since I was 10. After all these years, I still wasn't sure what had led him to drink. My mother hadn't talked about him much in the intervening years. I knew he had had career disappointments, but I wasn't sure whether the job setbacks caused the drinking or vice versa.

What I did remember were the late-night shouting matches that would awaken me at all hours, followed by the occasional breaking of dishes or glassware, and one time even furniture. What I had always wanted to forget was that fateful night when he crossed the line into hands-on violence against my mother. The tirade had begun routinely enough, with one too many drinks and a profanity-laced diatribe about how his exceptional talents had been overlooked at work.

My mother had said something in response that I hadn't been able to decipher, and suddenly I had heard a loud smack followed by running footsteps, then my mother's breathless voice. "My husband just hit me. I need a policeman here now! Yes. 422 Evans. Please hurry!"

I never got the full story. By the time the police were done talking to the two of them, it was morning. Apparently he had been taken before a judge, who had given him the choice of moving out or going to jail. He chose the former. He took his belongings the next day while I was at school, and I hadn't seen him since.

I did have some shadowy memories of him spending time with me when I was very young. I vaguely recalled holding his hand at a carnival when I was no more than four or five. He had taken me to a baseball game once. But by the time I was about eight years old, the alcohol had become his constant companion.

I took immense pride in the fact that I had risen above the troubles of my childhood to make a success of myself. There was no way I would ever allow a crutch like alcohol – or anything else – to get in the way of my career goals.

The last my mother had heard, dad had been living in Fairview, just 25 miles south of Franklin. But from the moment I had arrived and begun working for the Mirror, I had made up my mind I wasn't about to pay that drunk a visit after what he had done to my mother and me.

"Evan." Paige's voice snapped me out of my dark remembrance.

"Yes?"

"I'm going to step out for a while. Please spend some time thinking about what I just told you. He knows everything about you – every moral blemish, every selfish motivation – and yet desires to pardon you. In fact, in spite of all your shortcomings and your rejection of his authority, he loves you."

I wanted to find out *how* a pardon could be granted, but I didn't get the chance. With his stunning pronouncement, Paige was out the door, once again leaving me alone with my thoughts. This time I had much more to contemplate. *He wants to pardon you. He loves you.* That one resonated again. *He loves you.*

Until my arrival at Lawson Penitentiary, I had not wept since my father had left home. But now, once again, I could not stop the tears from flowing. I lay down on the bed and, for the first time since I was a young boy, cried myself to sleep.

# 5

The sound of the alarm clock jostled me awake. The clock said 6:30. I wondered if I would be facing the judge today.

Wait a minute. Where was I? I sat up. It was my own alarm clock that had awakened me. I looked around. Could it be? Yes! I was in my own bed! This was my apartment. It had all been a horrible nightmare! Never had I felt such a sense of sweet relief.

I jumped out of bed. I was free! No prison, no judge to face, no warden to deal with. I looked around. There was my laptop on my desk. There was the Sunday paper scattered on the floor by my bed. I looked on the wall. My Excellence in Investigative Journalism plaque was right where it belonged, as were my diploma from Relman and my Certificate of Appreciation from the middle school. I turned on the TV and looked at the scroll line. It was Monday, April 10th. Everything was as it should be. It was my last week on the job in Franklin. I would be starting at the Observer in one week. All was right with the world!

I had had some bad nightmares in the past, but this one was the worst. It was hauntingly realistic, no matter that it never could have happened in real life. People simply do not go to death row for exaggerating…or adultery, or embezzlement, or even for selling drugs. Now that I was awake, I laughed at the silliness of it.

I remembered a dream I had had years ago where I seemed to know, in the midst of the dream, that it was, in fact, a dream. That certainly had not been the case this time. Sure, it defied logic for me to be locked up on death row, but it had seemed so real that even now, back in the land of the wide awake, I was tempted to take a drive out 58 to see if there really was a penitentiary.

After showering and dressing, I stepped outside. It was so refreshing to breathe the precious air of freedom that I decided to celebrate. I would buy myself a sugary breakfast and eat at Woodland Park before heading over to City Hall to thank the city manager.

I grabbed two sprinkled donuts and a coffee and headed to the park. It was a beautiful spring morning, sunny and mild. I sat down at a picnic table and took a bite of the first donut. It was great to be alive.

One thing I had always appreciated about my nightmares was that the details would quickly fade. I rarely remembered them by the time I was done with breakfast. I was hoping last night's would be no exception. It had been quite a doozy. Indeed, I had never had such a bizarre dream in all my life.

I started thinking about that crazy character, Paige. I wondered if he represented someone I knew. Did I know anyone who looked like him? Did I know anyone who thought like him? No. But then I started remembering some of the things he had said to me. He had actually accused me of being not a good person...and I had started to believe it! I would be sure to tell Tom about this so we could have a good laugh together.

But wait. Tom's accident had not been just part of a bad dream. It really had happened. I remembered what Paige had told me about his accident. Could that possibly be true? Could it be that his death really was caused by someone under the influence? Thinking of Tom's passing made me no longer feel much like celebrating.

I finished the second doughnut and tossed the bag in the trash, grabbed what was left of my coffee and drove over to City Hall.

Becky, the receptionist, was at her post as always. "Good morning, Becky. How was your weekend?"

"Hey, Evan. Mine was good. How about yours?"

"Uh, it was okay, I guess." I wasn't about to burden Becky with the contents of my dream.

Her brow furrowed. "Hey, isn't this your last week with us?"

"Yeah, it is."

"Well, we're sure going to miss you around here."

"Thanks." Becky was nothing if not polite. "Hey, is Mr. Haskins in?"

"Yes, but he's in a meeting right now. Do you want to wait, or come back later?"

"I can wait a little while. Any idea how long it will last?"

"No, not really."

"I don't have an appointment. I was just hoping I could catch him for a short visit. I'll tell you what. I'll wait a few minutes and then come back later if the meeting goes long."

She smiled. "Okay, sounds good."

I went and sat down and watched people milling about in the lobby. Some were city employees. Others were residents taking care of business of one kind or another. I noticed a couple of people stop at the counter and drop their water bills in the slot. That reminded me I'd be getting my deposit back when I got my water shut off at the apartment. I would in turn use that to get the water turned on at my new place in the capital. I regretted that I had not taken the time to find a place yet. I would have to stay in a motel for a few days next week.

I glanced out the back entrance and saw some construction workers carrying 2x4s for the expansion project at City Hall. Part of me would miss Franklin. It was a fairly small city, but it was on the rise.
    As I sat back in the chair, I began to get lost in thought. The vivid memory of last night's dream would not escape me. Try as I might, I couldn't stop thinking about Tom and wondering about the circumstances of his death.
    My mind then began to wander to other aspects of the dream — the people I had interviewed, the mysterious lawgiver/judge, as well as the things the warden had said to me. Dream or no dream, I could not believe how I had allowed myself to give in to self-doubt. Does one have control over his thoughts in a dream? Probably not...yet I couldn't help but feel disappointment with myself for buying into the warden's argument. Now that I was awake, I once again felt quite comfortable with my moral compass.
    At that moment I glanced down and saw a brochure for Franklin College. In an instant, my mind was flooded with thoughts of Relman and the warden's accusation in my dream. My stomach began to knot as I realized that that aspect of the dream had been true.
    Wait...of course, that was it! My subconscious mind had been troubled by that all these years, and the guilt finally came out in the form of a dream. Oh, wouldn't Freud have loved this! That explained everything.
    It reminded me of a story Ralph had told me at the office a few months back. I was surprised to remember it since I usually tried to tune him out. Ralph said he had had a recurring dream of driving up a steep slope, and finally it got so steep that the car started falling backward. Each time the dream would scare him awake before the car landed. Then one time he had been visiting a family member out of state when he was driving through a residential neighborhood and came upon the steepest road he had ever seen — only

two blocks long, but astonishingly steep. There were signs announcing that trucks and buses were not permitted. He felt he had to try it. After his car successfully reached the top, he never again had that dream. Maybe for me the opposite would be true – instead of a real event stopping an ongoing bad dream, maybe in my case a bad dream would help expunge my real-life — until today, latent — guilt.

But instead my conscience started weighing on me at an even deeper level. That college application was not the only lie I had ever told. Indeed, I frequently used flattery to procure an interview or told subtle fibs to get people to answer difficult questions. In fact, on at least one occasion that sprang to mind, I had added a fictitious little twist to my newspaper story to make it more interesting as well as fulfill a personal agenda I had in mind for that particular story. Sure, I knew the truth was important, but I had reasoned that it never hurt anyone to do a little embellishing to make an important point or just for the sake of making a good story better.

Okay, that had to be it. That must have been the reason for the dream...not just my college application but my generally shaky relationship with the truth. It was nice to see that my college psychology class hadn't been a complete waste of time. Perhaps now I could put the dream behind me once and for all.

I sat quietly for a moment trying to turn my thoughts to another subject, but my nagging conscience wasn't going to let me off the hook that easily. I started thinking of my day-to-day interactions with people, unconnected to my role as a journalist. How often had I told lies to others? More than I could count. Why? To flatter them or to protect my reputation or simply to get my way. Into my brain rang the warden's words from my dream: *"You're self-centered."*

Oh, why had I had that horrible nightmare? Here I was at a great time in my life, days away from climbing a big rung on the career ladder, but now there was what felt like a giant spike of guilt trying to pierce my chest. Sure, my conscience had been bothering me in the dream, but I had hoped those feelings would have dissipated by now. The nightmare was still haunting me, hours after waking up. I began to dread going to bed that night. What if somehow the dream continued when I fell asleep?

\* \* \* \* \*

Suddenly a loud noise interrupted my brooding. I looked outside. One of the workers had dropped a stack of lumber. A kind soul ran over immediately to help him with it. It was at that precise moment that I experienced one of the greatest frights of my life, one that would be etched in my mind forever. My eyes grew wide as saucers as I looked at the man helping with the wood. He looked exactly like the young Hispanic man in my dream! It was as if I were seeing a ghost. I literally began to shake. What was happening? I turned away, hoping the city manager's meeting would end so I could escape into his office. It seemed that my dream was following me.

I looked back outside, and the young man was smiling warmly as he finished helping the worker with his load. But wait...now he was moving toward the door and about to walk into the building! I spotted a green water department envelope in his hand. He was coming to pay his bill.

I considered sneaking out the back door. It would be too much to handle if he somehow recognized me. I quickly started recollecting the details about the guy in my dream. I tried to remember his name. Miguel – that was it. I recalled that he was very depressed. He had been filled with regret over his anger problem.

"Evan?" I nearly jumped out of my skin at the sound of my name. I looked up. It was the receptionist. "Mr. Haskins' meeting is wrapping up in a minute, so I'll tell him you're here."

I stood up, anxious to get into Haskins' office, relieved that my escape had come just in the nick of time. But then suddenly I stopped and took a fuller measure of my impending crisis. I began to wonder if someday I would, in fact, regret not speaking to this gentleman. Perhaps what I needed for the nightmare to end was not to elude him but to actually talk to him face to face. I took a deep breath and tried for a moment to think calmly and rationally. There had to be a plausible explanation for this. Maybe I had seen him around before and that was how he ended up in my dream. I had to make a split-second decision. I looked at him, then at Becky.

"Could you tell Mr. Haskins I'll drop by later, Becky?"

"Sure, no problem."

By this time the man was already leaving the counter and heading back toward the door. I walked over to him. He looked at me and smiled. That was certainly a notable difference. Miguel never would have smiled.

I wasn't sure how to begin. "Excuse me, I'm sorry to bother you, but you look familiar. Your name isn't Miguel, is it?"

He maintained the same glowing expression. "No, my name's not Miguel, my friend." I was relieved to hear that. Unlike Miguel, he had no accent.

I cleared my throat and asked another question. "This may sound strange, but do I look familiar to you?"

He looked me over. "No. Have we met before?"

If I mentioned the dream to him, he would think I was crazy, so I steered clear of it. "No, I guess we haven't. May I ask your name?"

"Sam. Sam Rojas. What's yours?"

"My name is Evan Jamison. It's nice to meet you." I extended my hand, and he grasped it firmly. He was still looking buoyant. I wasn't sure how to proceed with this conversation. With an even tone I said, "You do look a lot like someone I once met, but now that I've spoken with you, I can see you don't have anything in common with him at all."

He flashed another grin. "Well, to be honest with you, I don't feel like I have much in common with myself."

I had interviewed a lot of people, but that may have been the single strangest thing I had ever heard. "Oh? What do you mean?"

"Let's just say my life is a lot different than it used to be."

"How so?"

He gushed. "I've been pardoned, my friend. I'm free!"

I was dumbfounded. *Pardoned.* I tried to keep a steady expression. "What was that?"

"I said I've been pardoned."

"Were you released from prison?"

"Yes, but not the kind of prison you're thinking of."

This was obviously going to be a fascinating conversation.

\* \* \* \* \*

My mind was racing. This wasn't another dream, was it? No, I was very much awake. I was determined to give Sam the appearance that this was a regular conversation, even though for me it was anything but. I hoped he didn't think I was staring at him, such was the resemblance between him and the character in my dream. I was relieved to observe that while he had a couple of tattoos on his arms, there was no dragon on his neck. At least he wasn't completely identical to Miguel.

I needed to know what he meant, but still did not want to appear over-anxious. "Aren't people normally pardoned after they go to prison?"

He was still smiling broadly. "Do you have a couple of minutes? I'd love to explain what I mean. I've got the day off, so I'm not in any hurry myself."

"Sure, I've got time," I said as casually as I could. Inside I was dying to hear what he had to say, even if it took hours.

"Something happened to me about six months ago that changed my life. I met someone who told me something I'd never really thought about before."

"Oh? What's that?"

"I was created."

I bristled. If I had been having this conversation 24 hours earlier, I would have politely excused myself and walked away. Creationists, in my mind, were science-hating zealots who should be avoided at all costs. But after last night's dream, and seeing Miguel's look-alike in front of me, those words did not repel me.

Sam then raised his eyebrows. "How about you? Do you believe you were created?"

Since my conscience had already been plaguing me about my struggle with truth-telling, I decided not to stretch it this time. "I guess I haven't really thought about it much." That was an honest answer.

"Oh, you should think about it, my friend. It's an amazing thing to realize that the same one who created the earth and the sun and the moon and the billions of stars also created you….in his own image, no less."

After what I had been through, part of me was beginning to hope that was true, but I was more interested in getting back to the pardon issue. "That's nice, but what did you mean a minute ago about being pardoned?"

"Sorry, what was your name again?"

"Evan."

"Evan. I'll get to that in a minute, Evan. First let me say this. I lived my whole life not understanding I had been created and who my maker was. That's kind of strange, if you think about it."

I shrugged my shoulders. "Oh? How so?"

"Well, I mean, you know, you'd think we, as created beings, would want to know the one who made us. But most people just aren't interested." He shook his head. "I know I wasn't."

I didn't want to be adversarial, but I could think of at least one good reason the interest wouldn't be there. "Well, if there is a creator, it would be a lot easier to know him if you could actually see him."

"Yeah, that's what I used to think. But I've learned two things about that. First of all, I was so wrapped up in my own little world that I never bothered to notice that there's evidence of him all around, even without seeing him."

"Oh?"

"Well, think about it. Can you see the wind?" He glanced around.

"Sure."

"Oh, really? You can see the actual wind?"

I was struck by the simplicity of his argument. "I guess not."

"You see what the wind does, but the wind itself is invisible. Okay, let me ask you another question. What time is the sun going to set on, let's say, August 22nd, 2215?"

I gave a puzzled expression. "Two centuries from now? I wouldn't know."

"Well, you could. All you need to do is check the Internet. Our solar system is so orderly that they know when the sun will rise and set as far into the future as you'd care to know. Isn't that amazing? I mean, we learned in grade school that the earth moves in two ways – it rotates on its axis and it orbits the sun. I never gave that a second thought. But how awesome is that? Our creator placed this earth at just the right distance from the sun, then started it spinning around and moving it through space, but he did it in a way that we don't even notice it...even though we're traveling thousands of miles an hour! The only evidence that it's moving is that the sun slowly rises and moves across the sky every day, then sets, like clock work. Oh, and of course we can also tell because of the movement of the stars and the moon. It's like he's waving a giant banner in the sky saying, 'I made this, and I made you, and I want you to believe in me.' But I was so caught up in my own little world that I never bothered to notice, and most other people don't either."

I was just about to interject, but he barely stopped to take a breath before continuing. "And have you ever looked at a satellite picture of the earth? How beautiful is that? That's because the creator is the source of beauty. Mountain lakes, ocean sunsets, canyons, rivers...he made 'em all."

Finally I had an opportunity to speak. "Now that you mention it, I must admit I've always taken those things for granted. But you still haven't answered my question."

He put his hand on my shoulder reassuringly. "Don't worry, I'll get to that. Keep in mind, all this is pretty new to me, so I don't claim to have all the answers. But here's the second point. One thing I've learned is you wouldn't want to see him with your own eyes even if you could."

"Oh? Why is that?"

He hesitated for a moment, seemingly to dramatize his point. "Because he's perfect."

"Well, if he's perfect, wouldn't he want to be seen?"

"Do you know any perfect people, Evan?"

"No." I started to laugh. "Do you?"

"I do now!" He too let out a laugh. "But I haven't seen him. See, one thing I've learned is that the creator is morally pure, and we can't even look at him because we're not pure. In fact, he cannot even have the slightest imperfection in his presence. That poses a problem, because one day every one of us is going to stand before him and give an account for our moral failings."

Again I remembered the feeling from my dream. By its end, I very much wanted to meet the judge, but was also frightened to do so because he had demonstrated that he somehow knew my inward flaws. That was precisely how I felt right now. I desperately wanted to know that there was perfection somewhere in the universe, but was equally afraid to encounter it.

\* \* \* \* \*

Sam glanced out the door and said, "Would you like to continue this outside? If you have to be somewhere, I understand, but I'd love to keep talking."

If he had the time, I had the time. But I still wanted it to seem casual on my part. "Yeah, that'd be okay."

We walked out into the bright sunshine. I felt the sun's rays glistening on my skin, which reinforced his observation about its subtle movement across the sky. He stopped on the sidewalk, looked up and flashed another smile while extending his arms upward. "It's great to be alive, isn't it?" He then looked at me. "You know, I didn't used to think that. In fact, there was a time when I thought suicide wasn't a bad option."

I could not hide the surprise from my face. "I find that hard to imagine."

"No, it's true. I had a pretty messed-up childhood. My dad drank a lot." That certainly caught my attention…we had something in common. "He used to hit me all the time. I tried to find an escape. When I was 13 I started smoking pot. When I was 15 I was using coke, and by the time I was 17 I was addicted to crack."

Maybe we didn't have that much in common after all. Unlike him, I had managed to resist going down that path. I couldn't help but think of my dream and the possibility a user may have caused my cousin's death. I began to feel a sense of discomfort with this guy. Maybe he was capable of doing something like that. Then again, from what I could tell, he was no drug user now. In fact, he seemed far from it. I decided to keep listening.

"My drug use led me to do a lot of other bad stuff. I'll spare you the details, but I hurt a lot of people. I wanted to change, but I couldn't. I was so full of shame that I started thinking about killing myself. But then I met this guy. His name is Mike, and now he's like a brother to me. He told me that I was created by a perfect, all-powerful being. At first I got upset, because I thought if he was all-powerful he should have stopped my dad from hurting me. But then I realized that I had hurt people too, and I couldn't blame anyone else for that but me. My dad was responsible for his own actions, and so was I."

I was struggling mightily with what I was hearing. Part of me couldn't help but associate Sam with the drug user Paige told me about in my dream, but another part of me was astonished at the man in front of me. I could scarcely believe he was the same person as the one he was describing. Now I was beginning to understand what he meant when he said he had little in common with himself.

Sam continued. "Mike shared with me that there was no way I could make things right with my creator. I was guilty of breaking his moral laws."

I had to consciously keep my mouth from dropping open. "What did you just say?"

"I said I was guilty of breaking his moral laws. I was guilty because he had created me and had the right to tell me how to live, but I had done things my way. Since he was perfect, what he said was right, but I chose to do the wrong thing instead. Talk about arrogant!" Sam looked straight at me. "And since he was my creator, he was prepared to give me justice for rejecting his rightful authority and going my own way."

"What is justice for that?"

"Permanent separation – not only now, but even after my physical death. We all live on after death, you know." No, I did not know that. "I could not enter his presence, because he is perfect. It would actually violate his nature to have imperfection in his presence."

I jumped in. "I assume you're talking about heaven. You're saying you couldn't go to heaven after you died?"

He nodded. "Exactly. But it's not just being kept out of heaven. Since he's just, he also would have to punish me. If he didn't, then he wouldn't be a very just judge, would he?"

"Wouldn't separation be sufficient punishment?"

"That's a good question. How about a murderer? Do you think a murderer should spend eternity floating on a cloud somewhere – just not in his creator's presence?"

Immediately my mind flashed back to the murderer/drug dealer in last night's dream and his complicity in my cousin's death. "Okay, I'll grant you that. But most people don't commit murder."

"Well, most people don't physically kill someone, that's true. But the creator's standards are a lot higher than ours. For example, according to his standard, if you hate someone, you're essentially guilty of murder in your heart because it's as if you wished that person was dead."

I thought about all the people I had had ill feelings for over the years, but I still wasn't ready to buy his argument. However, he hadn't finished making his point.

"Let's take something simpler. Suppose you had 100 parking tickets that you never paid, and they finally caught up with you. You went before the judge and said, 'I'm sorry, your honor, I didn't mean it.' Now let's say the judge looked down from his bench and said, 'Hey, listen, I understand. You were probably just having a bad day...all 100 times. I forgive you, and I'm going to let you go.' You might be happy about that, but what does that say about the judge?"

I thought that over for a moment. I was starting to understand his point. "I guess he wouldn't be a very good judge."

"Exactly. And here's the thing. When we commit sins against our creator, we think of them like individual parking tickets. They seem like no big deal to us. But to him, they are very serious offenses, because we're basically saying, 'Take a hike. I'll follow my own rules.' And by the end of this earthly life, we have millions of parking tickets. And we don't care, because we think we're moral free agents and we determine what's right and wrong. But we didn't create ourselves! We are dependent creatures. We were created by someone who is very powerful and also very holy, and whether we like it or not, we're accountable to him. But the problem is, our human nature is in rebellion against him. In our natural state, we don't want him telling us what to do. As a just judge, he has to respond to that. Since he exercises perfect justice, he cannot leave those things unpunished. As a just judge, he can't say, 'Oh, that's okay. No big deal. I absolve you.' Our sins have to be paid for."

I had never heard anything like this...except, of course, in my dream.

Sam continued. "See, deep down, people know when they're doing wrong, but they do it anyway. Eventually they get so used to it that they harden their hearts and convince themselves it's okay, and besides, even if it's wrong, the big Grandfather in the Sky will forgive them anyway. But I'll tell you something, Evan. Even after I had been using for years and years, I still knew deep down that it was wrong and I deserved to be punished for it."

That begged an obvious question. "If this guy told you there was no hope for you, why are you so happy now?"

Sam grinned from ear to ear. "That's the good part. It's the explanation to what you asked me about earlier. It's because he pardoned me."

I then instinctively uttered the same phrase I always use when not fully comprehending what someone says: "I beg your pardon?" The pun was lost on me, but not on him. He started to laugh. "No, I begged *his* pardon...and got it!"

I shook my head. "You're losing me, Sam."

"Let me explain. I didn't understand at first either. When Mike told me, it seemed too good to be true. Listen to this. He told me that in spite of my rebellion, in spite of all the terrible things I had done, my creator still *loved* me." I shivered. It felt as if there were an echo in my head from the night before.

He continued. "There was no hope for me to make myself right with him. Don't get me wrong — there was still hope, but it wasn't hope in myself. The hope came from outside of me. It came from him. He did something for me I couldn't do for myself." He chuckled. "I still get goose bumps when I think about it. It's amazing."

"What?" It was becoming difficult to pretend any longer that I was less than intensely curious.

"Since he loved me, he sent someone to take my place — to bear my punishment."

"Who?"

"Somebody very special to him – his own son. His own son took the penalty for me."

It began to dawn on me who he was talking about. My mother had taken me to church a few times when she started having trouble with Dad, and I had distant memories of it. "Are you referring to Jesus Christ?"

"I sure am!"

Again I had an instinct to walk away. For years I had been convinced that anyone who believed in Jesus Christ was either hopelessly naïve or a right-wing wacko, or both.

The Bible contained cute stories suitable for grade school kids, but it had no relevance in the real world, especially in the 21$^{st}$ century. But somehow this was different. I was now hearing it explained in a new way...and, powerfully, by a person who had undergone a radical change.

He continued. "There's no one like Jesus. He loved me so much, he died in my place. He took the death penalty for me."

Did he really say "death penalty"? For all intents and purposes, this guy was declaring that he had been on death row. Obviously that was why he chose the word "pardon."

He looked at me and said, "Would you like some gum?" He pointed to the far corner of the parking lot. "I've got some in my car."

"Sure."

As we stepped off the sidewalk, my Debate Club experience brought forth another question. "You said the creator is just. So where's the justice in somebody else dying for you? Sounds to me like he was a victim."

He stopped and turned to me. "Great question! It wouldn't have been just if Jesus had been an unwilling participant. But he was very willing. More than once he told his followers that he was going to suffer and die. He knew it was going to happen, but he kept right on going. He did that for me" – he then looked me straight in the eye – "and for you, Evan."

A strange feeling began to come over me...an odd combination of discomfort and hope.

A somber expression formed on Sam's face as he shifted gears. "It's sad. A lot of people think God is unaware of their problems, or worse, that he doesn't care. But Jesus can relate to people's suffering because he's been through more than anyone. He spent three years basically homeless, at the end of which he got arrested, faced a kangaroo court, was tortured, and then suffered the worst form of execution ever devised. Jesus can identify with us because he's experienced the worst form of anguish. And he did it for one primary purpose: So we would have the opportunity to get that pardon. We needed a perfect substitute to take our place, and he was it."

His face brightened. "But that's not all, Evan. He died, but he came back to life. He's alive! And he's proved it by setting me free from my own personal prison. I have no need for drugs. I have no interest in drugs. It's gone. When the Son sets you free, you are free indeed! I was using drugs to chase away the pain in my life, but what I was really doing was finding a weak substitute for the only thing that could bring me true peace — a relationship with my creator. Mike taught me a new word — 'reconcile.' That means two people getting their relationship fixed after having a really bad disagreement. In this case, the one who made me did nothing to cause the disagreement, but he did all the reconciling!"

# 6

My head was spinning. I had always prided myself on my antagonism toward organized religion. It was a myth and a waste of time. But now...now, mysteriously, something was beginning to burn inside me. Somehow, the way he was explaining this, it was both sensible and appealing. I found myself beginning to desire what Sam had. Joy was oozing through him. Still, he had raised a topic I had always found inconceivable: Resurrection. I had no desire to pop his bubble, because it clearly brought him great comfort, but I could not leave that one untouched.

We resumed our walk toward his car. "Listen, Sam, I'm really happy for you that you found something that has helped you get off drugs. And I'm impressed by what you said about Jesus dying for you. I really respect that. But you don't honestly believe he came back to life, do you? Be honest: Have you ever seen anyone come back from the dead?"

Once again, he stopped and looked at me. "I've never seen anyone physically come back to life, but I *know* he's alive! Do you really think I could change myself? I wasn't some casual drug user. I was hard-core – hooked. It wasn't till I called on Jesus that I was set free."

He pointed toward his car. "Come on, I still haven't gotten you that gum."

As we began to walk, I raised what I thought to be a good point. "Don't misunderstand me, Sam. I'm not devaluing your personal experience. I'll grant that that's your truth. It's just that" –

Sam again stopped in his tracks and politely but firmly cut me off. "My truth? There's no such thing as my truth or your truth, Evan. There is *the* truth, and we can either conform to it or not."

"So you're saying you believe in absolute truth."

"I sure do! Jesus Christ was a real human being who lived in time and space. He was born at a specific time and a specific place. He died at a specific time and place." He raised his eyebrows and gave a wry smile. "And, yes, he rose from the dead at a specific time and place."

Before I could counter-argue, he quickly continued. "Think of this, Evan. Jesus had 12 close disciples. One of them betrayed him, then killed himself. That left 11 others. At least 10 of the other 11 died a violent death. And the 12$^{th}$ was tortured and exiled."

"No doubt they were devoted followers."

"Yeah, but it had to be more than that. When Jesus was arrested, they all freaked out and ran. But something happened that transformed them from a bunch of cowards into a band of courageous men who paid the ultimate price for their devotion." I wasn't sure where he was going with this, so I gave a slight nod indicating my desire for him to continue.

"They didn't believe in just a philosophy or a religion. They believed in a man. When he died, they were crushed. They thought their hope was gone. But what changed them was when they saw him return to life again and when they received his Spirit. After that, nothing could stop them from telling other people about him and his resurrection. Even torture and death did not stop them. Sometimes people die for something they believe to be true that isn't true. In this case, if Jesus had not come back to life, every one of them would have died for something they knew to be a lie."

It was becoming increasingly difficult to remember that this man had once been a drug addict. I had never met anyone as convinced of his beliefs, or, for that matter, as persuasive in articulating them.

He went on. "There's another reason they were willing to suffer for him, Evan. They loved him. They had found something worth dying for — actually, *someone* worth dying for. The reason they loved him was because he loved them – and in a way that surpassed any normal human love. And when they saw him return from the dead, that confirmed the truth of everything else he had said — including that he had a kingdom that was not of this world. It was an eternal kingdom. When they saw him rise from the dead, they believed what he had said and were willing to do anything for his sake and for the sake of his kingdom." He paused, looking me squarely in the eye. "I am too."

I stood there and looked back at him. Clearly something extraordinary had happened to him, and his words in turn were having a deep impact on me. Whether he intended to or not, he had appealed to my emotions, then my intellect, and now I felt my will being drawn as well. Caught up in the moment, and with my limited understanding, I exclaimed, "I think I get it. Because you believe in the resurrection, you've been changed from bad to good!"

He took a moment to consider how to answer. "I wouldn't exactly put it that way. Oh, he's changed my desires, all right. I don't want to do bad stuff anymore. I'm still a long way from perfect, that's for sure, but the good in me – well, that's really him living his goodness through me." Once again I felt as if I were in an echo chamber. It seemed as if whatever was stated in my dream was eventually restated by Sam.

He then turned the spotlight on me with a question – it, too, similar to one I heard in my dream. "Do you consider yourself a good person, Evan?"

I scratched my chin. "I had always thought of myself that way. But some things have happened recently to cause me to, shall I say, rethink that."

He nodded. "That's a good place to be. The Bible says all have sinned and fall short of the glory of God. That includes you. It includes me too. In fact, I'm probably at the top of that list. I used to hate people. I blamed everyone for my problems. I blamed my dad. I blamed my enemies. Heck, I even blamed my friends. But I'll tell you something. Ever since I received my pardon, everything's different. Now I love people."

I wasn't ready to tell Sam about the dream, but decided to bring it up in an indirect way. "I was talking to a guy one time who seemed to suggest that the key to life is doing good for other people, but even then, it has to be with selfless motivation."

He was prepared with an answer. "Doing good is important, but salvation comes by faith in Christ alone. There's nothing you can do to help you get a right standing with God. There's nothing you can do to add to it or earn it. It's by grace. But when a person does receive God's forgiveness, his life will show it. It's like I was saying. I used to hate people, but now I want to help other people and show them his love. It's not to try to make up for the bad stuff I used to do. It's just to make him happy. He loves me, and all I want to do is love him back. The way I do that is with my actions. As a matter of fact, that's why I'm talking to you right now. A year ago I would have pushed you out of my way, but when you came up to me I was just busting to tell you about him. He has changed me completely. I have a new nature — his nature. I'm a brand new person. The Bible says, 'If anyone is in Christ, he is a new creation. The old has gone; the new has come.' Believe me, I'm not perfect — not by a long shot — but now he's living in me and I'm learning to give him more control and let him live through me more and more."

A car drove up and prepared to pull into the open parking space where we were still standing. Sam's back was to him, but I couldn't help but notice the driver's annoyed expression, which provided a sharp contrast to the attitude of the man with whom I was speaking. In fact, when Sam noticed the car, he turned around and smiled at the driver. "Sorry about that!"

As we stepped aside, he continued. "Getting right with God is based on one thing only: Trusting that Christ's death was the sufficient sacrifice for your sins. But the Bible also says that we will be judged by what we do. That's because our beliefs dictate our actions. If someone truly believes and understands they've been forgiven, love and joy will spring out of them. If they reject the truth – or do what a lot of people do, which is to just say a little prayer asking for Christ to come into their life, but never letting it carry from their heads to their hearts – then their actions will show they're not really one of his. Either they'll be so self-centered that they'll have no concern for other people, or else they'll do good things but with wrong motivations."

I thought about the kids I had tutored. What I had been told in my dream was correct. I had volunteered with less than pure motives. Now I understood why the warden had put so much emphasis on the inmates' actions. It was because their outward actions were a reflection of what was inside them.

By this time we had made our way over to his car. I glanced down and saw a bumper sticker: *"Everyone on the side of truth listens to me. Jesus."*

Such a provocative declaration prompted me to ask, "Is that a direct quote?"

"Yes, it's from the Gospel of John. Here, let me show you something." In an instant, he had in his hand a small Bible. "I can't get enough of this book. I read it every day." He quickly flipped through some pages. "Look at this. This is so great. John chapter 18, verse 37. *'Everyone on the side of truth listens to me.'* See?" He put his finger on it. Sure enough, there it was in black and white.

He got more excited as he turned the page. "Ooh, this is a good one. Check this out – John 14:6. *'I am the way, the truth and the life. No one comes to the Father except through me.'* See that? *'I am the truth.'* He doesn't just speak the truth. He IS the truth!"

I looked at the verse. That, too, was quite compelling. But then I re-read the last part. "*No one comes to the Father except through me.*" Once again I instinctively reacted. "That last part sounds kind of closed-minded to me."

"Yeah, some people think so. But truth by its very nature is limiting."

"How so?"

"What's two plus two? Any six-year-old knows the answer is four. What if somebody said they thought two plus two equaled five? Would it be closed-minded to tell them they're wrong?"

I smiled. "So are you equating your beliefs with mathematics?"

"No, I'm just trying to reinforce my point. Truth is objective, not subjective. Go step off the top of a tall building and see if gravity is a subjective truth." He laughed. "Seriously, if something is true, it doesn't make you arrogant to insist it's true…as long as you're humble about it. I've got an example for you. Take Christianity and Islam. They can't both be true."

"What are you talking about? Of course they can!" He seemed to be betraying a bias against Muslims.

"It's the resurrection issue again. Islam teaches that Jesus was merely a prophet and that he didn't die on the cross; he was taken up to heaven by God before he died. But the whole basis of Christianity is that he did die for our sins and rose again. So they can't both be true. If Islam is true, Christianity is necessarily false. And if Christianity is true, Islam is necessarily false. Both faiths make statements alleging facts. Either one is true or the other, or both are false. But they can't both be true. They're mutually exclusive. It's not closed-minded to say that. It's just a fact."

He shook his head and chuckled. "Ahmed didn't like it when I told him that. He got pretty mad at me."

"Who's Ahmed?"

"My co-worker. He was a devoted Muslim."

"What, did he quit his job to get away from you?"

"No, he still works with me. Why?"

"Because you used the past tense. You said he was a devoted Muslim, like he's not there anymore."

"No, he's still there. The reason I said 'was' is because he's not a Muslim anymore."

I felt the adrenaline kick up a notch. "What do you mean, he's not a Muslim anymore?"

"I mean he's now a Christian."

I was stunned. "How did that happen?"

"When Ahmed came to work there, I really liked him. He was a nice guy and a hard worker. One day we got talking about religion. I wasn't trying to pick an argument with him, but I made the same point I just told you about Christianity and Islam, that they can't both be true. As I said, he got pretty upset with me. But as time passed, I think he realized that I hadn't been trying to suggest that I was better than he was. I loved him and respected him as someone created in God's image. Well, anyway, to make a long story short, over the next few weeks he kind of softened his tone and we got along fine again. Then one day he told me something really nice."

"What's that?"

"He said he could see I had a close relationship with God. He said he had always wanted to know God in a personal way, but he was taught that God was distant and unknowable. Then one day we had lunch together and I asked him if I could show him some Scriptures, and he agreed. He believed what he read. That very day he placed his faith in Jesus. If you think I'm excited, you should see him! I've never seen anyone with more joy."

I was flabbergasted. I wanted to reject what he was telling me, given that it was the height of political incorrectness. But I could not ignore the goose bumps.

Sam could see that I was getting lost in thought. "Evan? One more thing about Jesus being the way. Remember what I said about him taking my punishment? Who else could have done that? He was the only one qualified. I needed a perfect substitute. If somebody was gonna cover my sins, he had to be sinless or else I would end up in the same boat. Jesus was the only qualified candidate. Only God – God the Son – could do that. Besides, if you're drowning and somebody throws a lifeline to you, you're not going to argue and say you want more than one choice of how to be rescued. You're just going to be thankful to have that lifeline."

That was a simple but profound observation. Before I could fully absorb it, his eyes lit up as a new thought came to him. "Ooh, it's even more than that. Hold on." He began flipping hurriedly through the pages. He seemed to have a little more trouble finding whatever it was he was looking for. Then he cried out, "Here it is! Look at this." I looked at the top of the page. It started with an E. I wasn't about to try pronouncing it.

He was giddy. "Look at this – Ephesians 2:1." *Eh-fee'- zhuns* – so that's how that word was pronounced. "'*As for you, you were dead in your transgressions and sins.'* See, it's more than just throwing a lifeline. It's like my sins made me spiritually dead and I was at the bottom of the ocean, and he came down and pulled me back to the surface, gave me mouth-to-mouth resuscitation, and brought me to life – as a new person. See, that explains why I just didn't get it before. I was dead to spiritual things. I couldn't understand them. But then he made me alive spiritually and everything made sense."

That led me to ponder a new and sobering thought: What about me? Was I spiritually dead?

His eyes began to mist up. "What's amazing is that he himself died in the act of rescuing me. He died so I wouldn't have to." He became hauntingly quiet. I stayed silent myself, moved both by his display of emotion and the things he was telling me. He shook his head. "I can't believe he did that for me. Look at this." He pointed at verse 4. *"'But because of his great love for us, God, who is rich in mercy, made us alive with Christ even when we were dead in transgressions – it is by grace you have been saved. And God raised us up with Christ and seated us with him in the heavenly realms in Christ Jesus, in order that in the coming ages he might show the incomparable riches of his grace, expressed in his kindness to us in Christ Jesus. For it is by grace you have been saved, through faith – and this not from yourselves, it is the gift of God – not by works, so that no one can boast.'*

His eyes moved from the page to me. "Evan, if you weren't aware of this, the word grace means undeserved favor."

He gave me a moment to weigh that before continuing. "Everyone on the side of truth listens to Jesus. The truth may seem offensive at first, because the truth says that you are facing eternal death, and you deserve it. But the truth also is that Jesus Christ was a real live person who entered time and space as a baby born in a manger and grew up to die on a cross. And the truth is that he is offering you eternal pardon through his shed blood."

He handed me the Bible and I looked at the words he had just read, then read them again. If this was true, it was indeed extraordinary. This meant that I, too, was dead in my transgressions and sins. But it also meant that Christ died for *me*.

* * * * *

My dream had shaken me badly. It had essentially challenged my sense of self. But now, wide awake, I was beginning to sense that what this person was telling me was the very thing I needed. It was a longing that had lay buried just beneath the surface, one I had done my best to suppress, because to acknowledge it would be to admit my own inadequacies and my need for something beyond myself.

Sam had no idea of the turmoil inside of me, because I had given him few cues of any kind. He sighed. "Evan, I realize you don't really know me. All you're seeing is the 'after.' You didn't see the 'before.' But I can tell you, it was terrible. I was a slave to drugs. All I thought about was my next high. The sad thing is, I was miserable, but I made no effort to turn away from it because I felt like I was in control of my life. Can you imagine that? I thought I was calling the shots, even as my life spiraled completely out of control. The truth is, I was actually the devil's slave, allowing him to control me."

The events of the last day and Sam's passion had helped convince me there likely was a God out there, but I remained doubtful about a devil. I just couldn't bring myself to accept the reality of some character with horns and a pitchfork. I decided to inquire about this alleged evil being. "Tell me, Sam, how does the Bible describe the devil?"

"Lots of ways. The prince of darkness. The thief who comes to steal, kill and destroy. But the description that comes to mind for me more than any other is that he's the father of lies." *The father of lies* – a sobering thought, given my own struggle with the truth.

"His first and foremost lie is that he doesn't exist. He convinces a lot of people of that." In spite of my skepticism, that made sense. What better way to undermine your enemy than to convince him you're not real?

"I'll tell you, Evan, I know exactly what Jesus was talking about when he called the devil the father of lies. I can look back and see it so clearly now. It was like he was a puppet master, pulling the strings in my life. I thought I was doing my own thing, but I was really doing what he wanted. I was believing his lies. All the while, he was trying to destroy me. I still see it all the time. I go visit people at the rehab facility. Most of them are buying the devil's lies hook, line and sinker."

"Like what?"

"Well, most of them have at least gotten to the point where they acknowledge they've got a problem. But they won't cry out to Jesus to deliver them. Some of them think what they've done is unforgivable. That's a lie. Some of them think they can get off drugs with their own effort. That's a lie too. We can't make it on our own. That's true for everybody, not just addicts. I just wish they could picture those puppet strings and realize they're under the devil's control, just like I was."

"So are you saying the devil made you do it?"

"No! I made my own choices. But he lied to me and convinced me I was king of my own little world and that my drug use was a valid lifestyle choice. But when I called out to Jesus, he cut those strings and set me free."

He started shaking his head. "You know what's sad? People reject their creator because they think *he's* the puppet master. But he's not a slave driver. He's a liberator! And I'm living proof!" It was both fascinating and deeply stirring to witness how energized he could get.

He went on. "You know what else is sad? There's lots of people out there who want nothing to do with God, who don't want him involved in their lives, but then when something bad happens, they complain that he didn't step in and prevent it. I know that from personal experience too."

He held out his hand and said, "Here, let me see the Bible. There's something else I want to show you from John." I obliged, and he quickly started flipping through the pages again.

"Before I read this, let me ask you a question. Are you more like a moth or a roach?" He burst into laughter before I could try to figure out what he was talking about. "Okay, let me explain. What does a roach do when you flip on a light? It tries to hide. Believe me, I know from personal observation. The way I used to live, I saw plenty of roaches! But what does a moth do when a light comes on? It flies toward the light. Okay, keep that in mind as I read this. Ready?"

"Yeah, go ahead." I was all ears.

"Okay. This is Jesus' words to a religious leader named Nicodemus. '*This is the verdict: Light has come into the world, but men loved darkness instead of light because their deeds were evil. Everyone who does evil hates the light, and will not come into the light for fear that his deeds will be exposed. But whoever lives by the truth comes into the light, so that it may be seen plainly that what he has done has been done through God.*'"

He looked up. "See, most people run from God because they don't want his bright light shining on them. The sad thing is, when they do that, what they're rejecting is love. If they stepped into the light, it's true that the light would expose everything bad. But if they would acknowledge the truth that they have sinned against their creator and ask him to take control, they'd be forgiven and made whole. It's like the old saying: Sunlight is the best disinfectant."

He shook his head. "Man, I used to be just like one of those roaches. God's light would start coming near me and I'd run the other way. I didn't want God to see me...as if he couldn't see me anyway! But then Mike explained that stepping into the light and accepting the truth about myself would set me free as I put my trust in Jesus because I'd be forgiven, not condemned. In fact, that's exactly what Jesus said to Nicodemus."

He pointed to a verse and read it out loud. *"'For God so loved the world that he gave his one and only Son, that whoever believes in him shall not perish but have eternal life. For God did not send his Son into the world to condemn the world, but to save the world through him.'* "

Sam looked at me with an expression of utter sincerity. "Evan, God doesn't want to condemn you. He wants to rescue you. He wants to bring you back from death and give you life. Here, look at the first thing Jesus said to Nicodemus." He again looked down at his Bible. *"'I tell you the truth, no one can see the kingdom of God unless he is born again.'* Born again means being born spiritually. The first birth is physical. The second birth is spiritual, where you become spiritually alive and get adopted as God's child."

I was beginning to understand why Jesus said, *"I am the truth."* These words were so...*true.* They were authentic. I thought again about the inmates in my dream. They were all like the proverbial roaches, stubbornly refusing to step into the light and accept the truth about themselves. The only exception was Miguel, Sam's look-alike. The warden said he had reached a milestone. Apparently Sam had reached that same milestone, only he had pierced the threshold and gotten to the other side and was now enjoying the light of day. His moth analogy was right on point, because it was obvious that he now wanted to be as close to the light as possible. As for me, I was beginning to feel mysteriously moth-like as well.

\* \* \* \* \*

I still was reluctant to talk about last night's dream, but could not resist posing a question. "Can I ask you something, Sam? Does God ever speak to people in dreams?"

"Definitely. There are lots of stories like that in the Bible. The Pharaoh in Egypt had a dream and a guy named Joseph interpreted it. The king of Babylon had a dream and Daniel interpreted it. Jesus' father Joseph had a dream. God spoke through dreams lots of times in the Bible." I was amazed at his knowledge, considering he was new to this by his own admission.

Sam's eyes then brightened once again and the corners of his mouth began to turn upward. "Hey, wait a minute. Why'd you ask me that?" He looked intently at me. "Did *you* have some kind of dream?" He was brimming. I had promised myself not to tell anybody about the dream for fear they'd think I had a screw loose, but that was before I met Sam. And after what I had been through, I also didn't want to lie in response to a direct question.

"Well, as a matter of fact, yes. I had a real strange one last night. You might think I'm crazy, but there was somebody in my dream who looked almost exactly like you. That was why I came over and talked to you."

He grabbed my shoulders. "Are you serious? Hallelujah! I told you he's alive! God still speaks through dreams!"

Only at that moment did I become finally and firmly convinced that mine was no ordinary dream. Perhaps I had wanted to deny the obvious, but now I realized that it required more than some kind of psychological explanation. It simply could not be a coincidence that Sam looked like Miguel, nor that my conversation with him was remarkably similar to the things the warden had said to me in my dream. Could it really be possible that the creator – as Sam described him, the maker of the entire universe – was trying to communicate with me? The thought left me simultaneously shaken and exultant.

Sam again looked me in the eye. "I don't know what you're thinking right now, Evan, but I will say this. If you believe what I've been telling you, your life will be forever changed. But remember" – his expression turned serious – "putting your faith in him strips you of every ounce of pride. I think that's why Jesus said anyone who comes to him must come like a little child. It's exercising simple trust like a little kid, which means it's very humbling. In fact, putting your faith in him means you abandon faith in yourself. The old you gets put to death. But then he'll raise up a brand new you, one who has right standing before his creator and can fulfill the purpose you were created for – to bring God glory and enjoy an incredible relationship with him that goes beyond what words can describe. That is what Jesus meant when he talked about being born again."

His expression grew even more intense. "Let me repeat something, just so it's clear. He won't accept you because you've tried to be good. He won't accept you because you're going to try harder to be good. But if you put your faith in Christ, accept you he will, because his son is good enough, and faith in him makes you acceptable in God's sight because all your guilt is nailed to the cross."

*Acceptable.* Previously I had never thought of myself as overly concerned about the acceptance of others, but today I had discovered the sobering fact that that was not the case. The warden in my dream was right: My lies had served as a way of getting others to see me a certain way, to accept me.

What I was certain I had never struggled with was accepting myself. I had always worked hard and done my best, and had accepted myself so well that I had become convinced I was better and smarter than just about everyone. But now I was beginning to grasp that what I needed more than anything was not self-acceptance but the acceptance of the one who made me. And this young man, my peer, who had had a similar childhood to my own but had taken a far different path, was telling me that my creator was offering to accept me.

In the span of 24 hours I had gone from the top of the mountain to the depths of despair. But now, speaking to a stranger in the stark setting of the parking lot of Franklin City Hall, I found my senses stirring as never before.

I looked at Sam and took a deep breath before making the simple declaration: "I believe it. I never thought I'd say that in a million years, but I believe it."

At the sound of those words, Sam's eyes began to swim. That in turn sparked me to weep just as I had in my dream. We embraced, our chests heaving from the tears. For the first time in my life, I was overwhelmed with the sense that I was truly loved...not with a fickle, what-have-you-done-for-me-lately human love, but with what I was now discovering to be the unconditional, unsurpassable, unquenchable love of my creator. The freedom I felt when I awakened from my dream was nothing compared to what I was now experiencing. The chains were loosed. I was beginning to get a taste of the peace I had seen in Sam.

# 7

When the tears finally subsided, I looked at Sam. "What happens now?"

He smiled. "Let me tell you what Mike told me six months ago. First, true belief is not just a change of mind. It's a change of direction. Jesus said, "Follow me." It's living your life under his control. It's going where he wants you to go and doing what he wants you to do."

"How will I know?"

"It's pretty straightforward. Start reading the Bible. The Bible was written by God and it has everything you need to know about God. Don't worry if you don't understand everything at first. God will help you. I would recommend beginning with the Gospel of John."

I had once thought that if the Bible were the only book in the world, I would still leave it unread. Now I found myself eager to open its pages and pore over it.

"The more you read the Bible, the more it will strengthen your faith." He shook his head. "It's sad that most people who are skeptical about the Bible have never bothered to read it." He certainly was right about that…I was Exhibit A. "I've only been showing you passages from the New Testament, but there's incredible stuff in the Old Testament too. It's the history of the Jewish people before Christ, but it's a lot more than just history. The whole thing points to the future arrival of Jesus as their Savior...sometimes in a subtle way, and other times it's spelled out directly. There were prophets who foretold future events, and one of them was a guy named Isaiah. In Isaiah chapter 53 he said that God would send a Savior who would be pierced, who would die for our sins, and who would come back to life. Well, here. Instead of me telling you about it, let me show you." He started turning the pages back toward the middle of his Bible.

"Listen to this. This was written about 700 years before Jesus was even born. *'Who has believed our message, and to whom has the arm of the LORD been revealed? He grew up before him like a tender shoot, and like a root out of dry ground. He had no beauty or majesty to attract us to him, nothing in his appearance that we should desire him. He was despised and rejected by men, a man of sorrows, and familiar with suffering. Like one from whom men hide their faces he was despised, and we esteemed him not. Surely he took up our infirmities and carried our sorrows, yet we considered him stricken by God, smitten by him, and afflicted. But he was pierced for our transgressions, he was crushed for our iniquities; the punishment that brought us peace was upon him, and by his wounds we are healed. We all, like sheep, have gone astray, each of us has turned to his own way; and the LORD has laid on him the iniquity of us all.'"*

He took a deep breath before continuing. *"'He was oppressed and afflicted, yet he did not open his mouth; he was led like a lamb to the slaughter, and as a sheep before her shearers is silent, so he did not open his mouth. By oppression and judgment he was taken away. And who can speak of his descendants? For he was cut off from the land of the living; for the transgression of my people he was stricken. He was assigned a grave with the wicked, and with the rich in his death, though he had done no violence, nor was any deceit in his mouth. Yet it was the LORD's will to crush him and cause him to suffer, and though the LORD makes his life a guilt offering, he will see his offspring and prolong his days, and the will of the LORD will prosper in his hand. After the suffering of his soul, he will see the light of life and be satisfied; by his knowledge my righteous servant will justify many, and he will bear their iniquities. Therefore I will give him a portion among the great, and he will divide the spoils with the strong, because he poured out his life unto death, and was numbered with the transgressors. For he bore the sin of many, and made intercession for the transgressors.'"*

For a moment I remained silent as the words sank in. Then I grabbed my pen and my reporter's notebook from my back pocket and prepared to write.

"I've got to read that again as soon as I get a Bible. What did you say that was?"

"Isaiah, chapter 53."

"And you said it was written 700 years before Christ's birth?"

"That's right."

"Incredible." I quickly jotted down the pertinent info – *Isaiah ch. 53; 700 years before birth.*

"There's more prophecies like that. Isaiah 7 says he would be born of a virgin. Zechariah 9 says he would come into Jerusalem riding on a donkey. Psalm 22 describes the crucifixion in detail. There's lots of examples like that."

I kept writing – *Isaiah 7, Zech. 9, Psalm 22.*

"When you pick out a Bible, make sure to spend a few extra bucks and get a study Bible. They have background information on every book, plus a lot of them have explanatory notes on some of the verses."

"Okay, great." I scribbled his instructions.

He waited for me to finish my writing. "Okay, ready for more? The next thing is to join the family of God."

This was a new term to me. "What do you mean?"

"I mean the church. You've probably noticed there's a lot of churches around." Actually, I hadn't; they had not really penetrated my radar screen. "You're welcome to come to mine, if you'd like."

"Well, as a matter of fact, I'm moving to the capital next week. I'm about to start a new job there." I suddenly felt a tinge of sadness at the prospect of moving away from my new friend.

"Well, I'm sure they have some good churches there. I would suggest getting a list of churches in that area. Maybe you could spend time checking out their websites. Then when you see one that appeals to you, go to a worship service. See whether the pastor gives lip service to the Bible or whether he really teaches it and is passionate about it. It's important to go to a church where they take the Word seriously. You also should pay attention to the atmosphere of the church."

It was obvious I had a lot to learn. "What does that mean – atmosphere?"

"It means how the people act. Are they excited to be there? Do they truly worship God, or just kind of sit there? Are they loving toward each other? Are they friendly toward you as a guest, or do they ignore you? In other words, see if they really live what they say they believe."

I smiled. "You know, I used to think churches were full of hypocrites, and now I'm about to go to one!" It also struck me that, up till now, I had been a hypocrite myself without ever realizing it.

Sam shook his head. "There are some churches that are loaded with hypocrites. You want to avoid them. You want to go where there's a community of people who know what they've been redeemed from and love God for it."

If it had people like Sam in it, I'd be quite comfortable.

"Oh, and once you've found that church, you should be baptized."

I had heard the term but didn't really understand what it meant. "What exactly is that?"

"It's real simple. It's publicly declaring that you are identifying yourself with Jesus Christ. It's also an act of obedience to God. The Bible says, *"Repent and be baptized."*

"Well, what happens? How exactly do you do that?"

"In our church, the pastor immerses you in water. It's symbolic. It represents Jesus' death and burial when you go down into the water, and his resurrection when you come back out of the water. And it shows that you have died to your old self and have been made a new creation. For me, it was an amazing experience. Mike was there alongside the pastor."

"Anything else?"

"Yeah. Pray. Talk to God. Be honest with him. He already knows everything about you, so there's no sense hiding it!"

I thought about the unseen judge in my dream. He had known me quite well. Still, I felt a bit hesitant. "I've never really prayed before."

"Well, now's a good time to start. Why don't you tell God how you're feeling and thank him for what he's done? Don't worry, I won't laugh…and neither will he."

Sam was right. It would be fitting for me to talk to my creator. I wasn't sure what to say, but I remembered his challenge to be honest.

I closed my eyes. *"Hello, God. Until today, I never thought I'd be talking to you in person. Maybe you didn't think I would either. I doubted your existence. I really had you figured wrong. I want to thank you for showing me the truth about you… and also about myself. I just want to acknowledge that you are pure, and I now understand that I'm not. I'm sorry for rejecting you all these years. I'm sorry for how prideful I've been. But I want to thank you for loving me in spite of that. Thank you for sending your Son to die for me. Thank you for forgiving me and giving me a second chance. I guess I should also thank you for last night's dream, because I'm quite sure you had something to do with that. Please help me to learn how to follow Jesus. Oh, and thank you for my new friend Sam."*

\* \* \* \* \*

It felt gratifying to say a real prayer for the first time in my life and to be confident that it was heard. The only problem was that I didn't quite know how to finish the prayer. So after I paused, Sam finished for me, letting out a hearty "In Jesus' Name! Amen!" He then gave me a bear hug.

He smiled and said, "Okay, there's still one more thing."

"I'm all ears."

"You need to show and tell."

I smiled back at him. "Okay, that's another one you'll have to explain to the newbie."

"First, you need to show Christ to people by how you live. You need to show them you're now one of his followers. It's like what we talked about before. If your faith is genuine, which I believe it is, it will naturally flow out of you through your actions." His face once again brightened as he opened his Bible. "I just remembered a story in the book of Acts."

I didn't want to admit that I had no idea whether he said acts or ax.

He found what he was looking for. "Here it is – chapter 16. Just read it yourself. Start at verse 16." He pointed out the small number which indicated the verse. "Read through verse 34." I noticed the correct spelling – "Acts."

I then read an extraordinary tale of two men, Paul and Silas, who had been arrested – I didn't fully grasp why – and mercilessly beaten. Then, late at night in their jail cell, they had somehow found the strength to sing and pray. That alone boggled my mind. But then, beyond that, there was a powerful earthquake that shook the bars loose. The jailer was about to kill himself – from what I knew of ancient Roman history, I presumed because he would have been executed or disgraced for allowing the inmates to escape, which seemed utterly unfair to me, given the circumstances – until Paul told him they were all still there. The jailer then became a believer and was baptized, and afterward cleansed their wounds.

I had mixed emotions after finishing it. Part of me was thrilled to read such a captivating story. Another part of me was chagrined that I had gone so many years dismissing the Bible.

I looked over at Sam and said, "That was amazing."

He laughed. "You got that right! It is amazing. Now you know why I love this book so much. What did you think of the jailer?"

"What a transformation! He went from treating those men like criminals to cleaning their wounds."

"That's right. That's what I wanted you to see. He showed Christ. He had a personal encounter with Jesus and it changed him on the spot. He took care of them in his own home. It was living faith."

I wanted to make an observation of my own, but was hesitant to do so since this was all so new to me, then decided it wouldn't hurt. "This 'showing Christ' – well, it seemed that Paul and Silas did so as well with their actions. In fact, it appears that the jailer never would have had the opportunity to 'show Christ' if they hadn't done so first."

"That's a great point! You're right." His expression then turned more somber. "Speaking of Paul and Silas, what happened to them shows something else you need to be mindful of. The Christian life is not a bed of roses. You will have hard times, I promise you. In some countries there are followers of Christ who are tortured or even killed for their faith. It's been that way since the first days of the church.

One thing you're going to learn, Evan, is that this world is no longer your home. You're going to start feeling like a foreigner, because you are now a citizen of heaven. And the world may treat you like a foreigner as well, because following Christ is countercultural. But that doesn't mean you should withdraw from the world. In fact, it's all the more reason to show Christ to others so that they can become citizens of heaven too."

The thought of people suffering for what they believed in was sobering. Ironically his words left me not only undeterred, but with a strengthened conviction that what I now believed was true. I had finally discovered something worth living for, which meant it was worth dying for as well.

I handed the Bible back to Sam. "Okay, so that's the 'show.' What about the 'tell'?"

"I'm glad you asked." He once again started flipping pages, but this time seemed to know exactly where he was going. In a flash he had found the right spot. "Here we go – back in the Gospel of John."

"You certainly seem to have a fondness for that one."

"Yeah, I do. That's the first book of the Bible that I read. I've read this particular story a bunch of times. It's one of my favorites. It's John, chapter 4. I need to explain a couple of things to you about it that Mike told me. It's a story about a woman in the region of Samaria. The Samaritan people were looked down on by the Jewish people because they thought of them as half-breeds and compromisers."

"Is this the story of the Good Samaritan? I've heard of that one."

"Different story."

"Sorry. Go ahead."

"Anyway, this woman was going to get water at the town well. When Jesus saw her, he started talking to her. It was unthinkable for a man in that culture to talk to a woman, much less a Jewish man talk to a Samaritan woman. Mike also told me that it was unusual for her to be getting water at that hour because it was the hottest time of the day, and most people got their water in the morning or evening. Plus the well was like a gathering place, so people wouldn't normally go there alone. But the story gives a reason why she might have been alone."

He was about to hand me the Bible again, but then said, "Hey, do you mind if I read it? I just love this story."

"By all means, go right ahead."

I then listened to a tale unlike anything I had ever heard. With a few helpful comments along the way from Sam, I learned of a woman who had hopped from husband to husband and had now settled on a cohabitational relationship — which sounded like a similar living arrangement to one I had experienced prior to moving to Franklin.

It was obvious why the woman had come to the well alone. She had been ostracized. Jesus, however, not only spoke to her, but revealed himself to her as the source of her greatest need. It was a poignant illustration of the transformation that had just occurred in me.

As the story began to wind down, Sam began to smile broadly. "Okay, listen to this. *'Just then his disciples returned and were surprised to find him talking with a woman. But no one asked, "What do you want?" or "Why are you talking with her?" Then, leaving her water jar, the woman went back to the town and said to the people, "Come, see a man who told me everything I ever did. Could this be the Christ?" They came out of the town and made their way toward him.'*"

Sam stopped reading and looked directly at me. "Hear that? That right there is the 'tell.' If she really was an outcast, that makes this even more amazing. She went and found the very people who looked down on her. She wanted to tell them about Jesus. That's something I've found to be true in my own life. I want people to experience what I've experienced, to believe what I believe. I can't help but tell people.

That's why I was so excited to get in a conversation with you. God knew what he was doing. My schedule just got switched this week. Otherwise we never would have met."

It occurred to me that I hadn't asked him what kind of job he had. "By the way, what do you do for a living?"

"I work in a warehouse. It's hard work, but I'm thankful for it."

That surprised me. "A warehouse, huh? Hey, don't take this wrong, but you don't strike me as a warehouse worker."

"Why is that?"

"You seem to have more of an interest in reading than the average warehouse worker."

"Well, keep in mind I was an addict until six months ago. I never graduated from high school. Your options are limited without a diploma. Besides, it's not like I'm some kind of book worm. It's just that I can't put the Bible down. I can't live without it. It also helps to have a friend like Mike to teach me. Plus I hear excellent preaching every Sunday. But to tell you the truth, I like my job. I believe I'm right where God wants me. I'm in the process of going for my GED, but I'm going to keep working there until God tells me otherwise."

I regretted making a judgment about his job. Apparently it would take time for some of my old ways to change.

There was a bit more left in the story. "Okay, I'm going to skip ahead just a little bit and read the end. *Many of the Samaritans from that town believed in him because of the woman's testimony, "He told me everything I ever did." So when the Samaritans came to him, they urged him to stay with them, and he stayed two days. And because of his words many more became believers. They said to the woman, "We no longer believe just because of what you said. Now we have heard for ourselves, and we know that this man really is the Savior of the world."'*

He looked at me. "There you have it – some examples of show and tell. That's what God wants you to do."

\* \* \* \* \*

I smiled as I contemplated what Sam had just read. What a story! I began to laugh out loud.

Sam smiled and said, "What?"

"I was just thinking. First of all, I can't get over the change I'm feeling. Until now the Bible meant absolutely nothing to me, and now I'm hearing these stories and it's making my heart jump. But something touched me about that story as you were reading it."

"What's that?"

"Well, it occurred to me that I was just like those townspeople. I would have been the first one to ostracize that woman. I've always had a tendency to look down on people. But the truth is, I was also just like her in a way. I was totally empty without even realizing it. I can see it so clearly now. Everything I did was a futile effort to try to fill the void."

Sam nodded. "Boy, that's so true of me. I was trying to find happiness in crack. But as I said, I didn't see the problem was with me. In my mind, I was the victim. It was everybody else's fault, especially my dad's. But then God showed me the truth about myself."

I couldn't resist posing a question about his father. "Does your dad know what's happened to you?"

"No, unfortunately he died four years ago."

"Oh. I'm sorry to hear that."

"Thanks. Believe me, I would give anything to have the chance to talk to him just one more time. I'd tell him what God has done for me. I'd tell him how much he hurt me, but I'd also tell him I forgave him. My dad had a lot of faults, obviously. I don't condone what he did to me. But I do forgive him. If God could forgive me for all the stuff I did, I could forgive my father."

He looked reflective. "But you know what? Even though it makes me sad that I'll never have the chance to have a real relationship with my dad, it's okay, because I've been adopted by my heavenly Father. He is the perfect father. In fact, the Bible says we can call him 'Abba,' which means 'Daddy.' He wants us to have an intimate relationship with him."

Once more I had a flashback. The warden had told me the judge wanted to be a father to me. At the time I had thought it quite strange.

I glanced at my watch. I had many more questions, but decided I didn't want to monopolize his entire day off. I politely told him I needed to get going. He said, "Okay, but there's one more thing I want to tell you about the greatness of Jesus."

"What's that?"

"Well, he's a lot of things. He's our Lord. He's our Savior. He's our older brother. He's our advocate. He's our king. But that's not all. He's also *the* King – the King of kings. There's been a lot of world leaders throughout history, and every one of them made mistakes. A lot of them were terrible dictators, like Hitler. But even the ones who were good leaders, their rule was only temporary. Look at presidents. What's the longest they can serve – eight years? Eight years! That sounds like a long time, but it goes by quick. Even if they do a great job, it's only temporary. It doesn't really change things. Listen to this Bible verse I memorized. It's Psalm 146:2-3. *'Do not put your trust in princes, in mortal men, who cannot save. When their spirit departs, they return to the ground; on that very day their plans come to nothing.'*

"People always think somehow things will get better... someday. It hasn't happened in 5,000 years, so what makes them think it'll happen now? As a matter of fact, things aren't getting better...they're getting worse. But Jesus is going to return and make everything right. Isaiah says, *'The government will be on his shoulders.'* Right now he rules in the hearts of his people. But the day is coming soon when he will return and visibly rule everything. The Bible says every knee will bow and every tongue confess that Jesus Christ is Lord. He will be the one perfect leader, and his rule will last forever. Until then, as I said, you are going to feel more and more out of place in this world. You are now a citizen of heaven."

A chill went down my spine. For all my frustration with our political system, this was precisely what I needed to hear. I had always believed, deep down, that the ideal leader was out there somewhere, and now I had discovered who he was. Better yet, and more awe-inspiring, I had spoken to him personally! Sam could have said nothing better to conclude our conversation. In fact, I strongly suspected that God himself had prompted him to say that for my benefit.

We embraced again. I thanked him for being generous with his time. We exchanged phone numbers, and I promised not to pester him with too many questions. He assured me it was okay to call anytime.

As I started walking toward my car, he gently grabbed my arm, "Evan, I've got something I want to give you."

"What's that?"

He held out his Bible.

"Oh, no, I can't take that."

"I insist. I want you to have it. This will hold you over till you get your own."

I still hesitated.

"Listen, I've got a larger one at home, and I can pick up another pocket Bible easily enough."

I decided it was an argument I wasn't going to win. I thanked Sam for the Bible and for his time. As I walked toward my car, I heard him call my name one more time.

"Evan!"

"Yeah?"

"I almost forgot. Here's that gum I promised you!" He ran over and handed it to me, a big smile on his face. We embraced one more time. I then walked to my car with a skip in my step.

# 8

As I settled into the driver's seat and turned the ignition, it occurred to me that I was changing after all, for I had an instinctive sense there were specific things for me to do – actions I never would have been willing to undertake before now.

First on the agenda was a trip to the office. When I arrived, I went straight to the desk of Ralph, the man I had looked down on from the day I arrived two years earlier.

"Hey, Ralph, can I talk to you for a second?"

Ralph continued typing for a couple of seconds and then looked up from his computer screen. "What's up, Evan? Last week, huh?"

"Yeah." I perched myself on the corner of his desk. "Listen, Ralph, I need to tell you something. I believe I owe you an apology."

Ralph raised his eyebrows in surprise and leaned back in his chair. "For what?"

"How can I say this? I haven't really respected you the way I should. I thought I was a lot better reporter than you."

"You are a better reporter than me. Everybody knows that!" He was being his usual pleasant self. "I think I'm okay at digging up information, but you're better at putting your stories into words than I am."

"Well, it's nice of you to say that, but you don't understand. It's not just that I thought I was better at this than you. I basically held you in contempt. I thought I was morally superior to you. That was wrong, and I'm very sorry."

"Well, since you're being honest with me, I'll be honest with you. I knew you felt that way about me."

"You did?"

"Sure. You didn't exactly hide it, Evan. Listen, you're a sharp guy and a great reporter, but humility has never been one of your strong points."

Had my arrogance been that obvious?

"But, hey, Evan, I appreciate you saying that to me. That was real gentlemanly of you. Why'd you tell me that, anyway? Just wanted to get it off your chest before you leave us?" He smiled broadly.

I then told him about my conversation with Sam and how I had placed my faith in Jesus Christ.

"Well, Evan, I must admit, that surprises me. You're the last person I ever figured would get religious. But I'm glad you found something that makes you happy. And don't feel bad about what you said before. I appreciate your honesty."

*Honesty.* I really was changing. I had managed to be completely candid and forthcoming...and it felt good!

Next on my internal to-do list was to speak with Dave Devlin, my editor. I walked over to Dave's door, which was open as usual. He was sitting at his desk, typing away. He looked up and gave me a smile. "Hey, Evan! Were you able to take care of some odds and ends today?"

I eased into the worn chair opposite him. "Well, not exactly. But I did have an eventful day."

"Oh?" He could tell I wanted to elaborate. "What happened?"

"I'll tell you in a minute. First I have a favor to ask of you."

"Sure. What do you need?"

"I was wondering if I could write an op-ed piece to thank the community for their kindness to me."

"I think that would be very nice, Evan."

"Well, it would also be somewhat confessional as well."

"Oh? How so?"

I took a deep breath. What I was about to tell him would be difficult, but I was confident it was what I was supposed to do. I had a lot of respect for Dave as a man of integrity who was an old-school stickler for accuracy. "Dave, I've taken a lot of pride in my work here. I've tried to be the best reporter I could be. In fact, I've tried too hard sometimes."

"What do you mean?"

"Well, one time in particular I added a little flavor to a story by including a few twists that weren't completely...truthful."

He sat up bolt straight and his eyes narrowed. "What?"

"I'm very sorry, Dave. It was wrong."

"I can't believe this, Evan. I trusted you."

"I know. Again, I'm very sorry."

"You need to tell me which story so we can print a retraction."

"Well, you may not find that necessary since I'm going to mention it in the op-ed. And it may comfort you to know that I didn't interview a fictitious person or anything like that. I never misquoted anyone."

"Well, I'm relieved you didn't make up your story out of thin air. But whatever it was, I need specifics."

"Well, remember that story I did on food stamp recipients?"

"Yeah."

"There was an elderly man I interviewed. I wanted people to sympathize with him, as well as support increases in the program, so I wrote that I could audibly hear his stomach growling and that he looked pale and was short on food. That simply wasn't true. He looked fine, and he actually had an adequate food supply."

I wasn't sure how he would respond to this. What I had divulged wasn't exactly a bombshell, but it still violated his code of conduct for the Mirror. He leaned back and put his hands together so that the tips of his fingers were touching. "You know, Evan, a lot of people would think nothing of that. They'd see it as poetic license. But you know as well as I do that a newspaper's reputation for accuracy is everything."

"Yes."

"Well, it was wrong, Evan. I'm disappointed." He shifted in his chair and intertwined his fingers. "Having said that, I would not recommend that you mention it in your op-ed."

"Why not?"

"If I had found this out sooner, it's possible I would have suspended you or even fired you. I can't tolerate tactics like that. But the fact that you've admitted it suggests to me that you don't intend to do it again."

He sat up and leaned toward me. "Evan, you're on the brink of starting a new job. If you put this before the public, the Observer may find out and withdraw their offer. Just promise me you'll never do this again!"

I thought about the Observer. Getting that job was what I had dreamed of and worked toward since the day I arrived in Franklin. I was still eager to take on my new responsibility, but now my priorities were decidedly differently. "Dave, I'm very grateful for your forbearance, and I appreciate your concern for my career. But I feel I must say this to the people of Franklin. And that's not all. I'm going to notify Craig Diehl at the Observer and tell him myself."

Dave shook his head. "What's gotten into you, Evan?"

Dave was skeptical about religion. Being a fair-minded editor, he did not carry a professional bias against Christianity, but on a personal level he had made comments from time to time indicating that he did not embrace faith at an intellectual level. He simply didn't believe it. Up until today, he and I had had a lot in common in that regard.

I decided to be as open as possible out of respect for him, so I proceeded to tell him about last night's dream. I knew he wouldn't believe it, but thought he deserved the whole story. Then I told him about my encounter with Sam and our conversation, and ultimately the radical step of placing my faith in Christ.

He reacted with quiet courtesy, as I would have expected. I imagined he was probably now relieved, under these new circumstances, that I was moving on, although he was too polite to ever say so out loud. What I appreciated was that he said he remained willing to have me write the farewell op-ed – in my own words, whatever I wanted to say.

After walking out of his office and over to my desk, I found myself praying again – thanking God for again giving me the courage to be truthful, then asking for help in my next encounter.

\* \* \* \* \*

The Capital Observer was considered the most prestigious paper in the state. Craig Diehl had been its editor for seven years. I had met with him twice in the interview process. He was absolutely driven, a Type A of the first order. He had a reputation as a tough but fair boss – like Dave on steroids.

The Observer's switchboard operator put me through. "This is Craig Diehl."

"Hi, Craig. This is Evan Jamison down in Franklin."

"Hey, Evan. Everything in order for your move?"

"Pretty much. How are things at the Observer?"

"Busy, busy. We're looking forward to getting your help. Hey, I've just got a couple of minutes. What's up?"

"Well, Craig, I really appreciate you offering me a job. But there's something I need to tell you."

He laughed. "Hey, you're not getting cold feet, are you? Don't worry, I think you're ready to hang with the big boys."

"No, that's not it. I just felt the need to tell you that I wasn't completely honest with you in my interview process."

"Oh? How so?" He sounded as if he were trying not to come across as overly concerned.

I then proceeded to share with him the same story I had told Dave about the liberties I had taken in my report on food-stamp recipients. He was quiet for a few seconds, which I wasn't sure how to interpret. It was a challenge trying to gauge his response without the benefit of being face to face.

"Evan, did you know we had a reporter completely make up a story a couple of years ago?"

"Yes, I remember hearing about that."

"Naturally, we fired him the instant we found out. So you're not telling me you made up any stories, right?"

"No, just a couple of embellishments."

"Well, that's a relief." Maybe he was okay with it.

"Why are you telling me this, Evan?"

"Craig, I've been looking forward to this job for a long time. I wanted to work for the Observer so badly, I could taste it. To be honest, part of the reason I juiced up that story was to help solidify my chances at being hired by you. It was actually one of the articles I sent as a sample of my work. But I had an unusual experience today. First, my conscience started troubling me about my truth-telling." Since I didn't really know him, I didn't bother explaining that a dream had been the catalyst. "Then I met somebody over at City Hall, a young guy who said he had been addicted to crack and that Jesus Christ had released him from his addiction. I'll tell you, the change in him must have been extraordinary, because he was the farthest thing from an addict I could imagine. That conversation had a profound effect on me."

Diehl laughed. "Oh, so you're telling me you found Jesus, huh?" It was obvious from his tone that he was being facetious. Thus he could not have expected my answer.

"As a matter of fact, I did."

There was silence. It seemed like minutes, but in reality it was probably only seconds. Finally he spoke. "Listen, Evan, I really am buried right now. I appreciate the call. Thanks a lot."

"Okay, Craig. Take care."

I had no idea what he was thinking. Apparently I still had a job, but couldn't be sure. I again said a prayer of thanks and prepared to tackle the next item on my new to-do list.

\* \* \* \* \*

I poured a cup of coffee and returned to my desk. It was time to write that op-ed to the community.

*A Farewell to Franklin - Evan Jamison, Mirror staff writer*

*When I arrived here in Franklin two years ago, I considered it nothing more than a stepping stone, just another rung on the career ladder. I did not regard this community as others did – as home.*

*To be sure, Franklin, like any community, is not without its share of problems. But all in all, this is a great community. I have met hundreds of people here, and the vast majority of them are warm, kind and hard-working. Volunteer opportunities abound. Neighborhood Watch associations are present all around town. Civic groups in the area provide important social and educational opportunities for children and youth.*

*I have enjoyed my time in Franklin. Unfortunately, I was so busy thinking of my next career move that I didn't take the time to enjoy it as much as I should. I was so preoccupied with covering the city that I didn't get to know the city.*

*I owe each of you an apology. Not only did I fail to appreciate the beauty of this community, but I also was at times less than honest with you. On one occasion, in a story on food stamps, I employed hyperbole in my writing, both to make the story more interesting and to feed my own desire to influence public opinion. I assure you, I never made up a story. My embellishments were very subtle. Nevertheless, what I did was wrong and I apologize.*

*I had no intention of telling you this. I was going to slip away to my new position at the Capital Observer without saying a word about it. But something happened to me in the parking lot of City Hall that has forever changed how I view myself and the world around me. I met a warehouse worker, no older than myself, who told me that he had once been addicted to crack cocaine but was released from its grip by Jesus Christ.*

*When I met him, I was already going through a crisis of conscience. I was becoming troubled by the ease with which I have so often told half-truths – not only in my column, but even more so in my day-to-day interactions with people — all in an effort to make myself look good to others. I finally decided to be brutally honest with myself, and now in turn I am being honest with you. I publicly acknowledge that I am a morally flawed person who has sinned against my creator, but I have received the forgiveness that can only come through Jesus Christ.*

*That may offend you. Until now, I would have been the first to take offense at that. I'm not telling you this to try to antagonize you but rather to speak truth to you. I feel I owe you that after what I've done. Now, as I prepare to depart, I ask your forgiveness for my arrogance and for not respecting you enough to always report to you with 100 percent accuracy.*

*I would like to thank my editor, Dave Devlin, for his cooperation in the publication of this piece. It is not without some risk on his part, because it may lead some readers to wrongly conclude that this paper is not trustworthy. Please rest assured that you can, in fact, trust the Mirror in spite of my past indiscretion.*

*Again, I thank you for your hospitality to me during my time in Franklin. I will never forget this place.*

I e-mailed it to Dave. Since he had pledged to print whatever I wanted to say, I believed he would keep his word. I glanced across the newsroom and noticed he was talking with a young woman at his desk, so I decided to go home and wait till I opened the next morning's edition to see if it was there or not.

Now that that task was completed, I was eager to start reading the Bible Sam had given me. When I arrived at the apartment, I stuck a frozen dinner in the oven and plopped down on the couch. Taking Sam's suggestion, I found the Gospel of John and started to read.

\* \* \* \* \*

I could see immediately why Sam liked John so much. It was very creatively written. *"In the beginning was the Word, and the Word was with God, and the Word was God. He was with God in the beginning."*
I especially liked verse 14: *"The Word became flesh and made his dwelling among us. We have seen his glory, the glory of the One and Only, who came from the Father, full of grace and truth."*
On I read, through the rest of chapter 1 and on to chapter 2. Then I came to chapter 3 and got the full context of what Sam had read to me earlier – the conversation Jesus had with the man named Nicodemus. Then I re-read the wonderful story in chapter 4 about the Samaritan woman whom Jesus met at the well.
The timer went off on the oven. I grabbed a hot pad, put the dinner on the counter to let it cool, then sat back down. I decided to be adventurous and do a little Bible exploring. I skipped ahead and found one of the letters written by Paul, this one called 1 Corinthians. In the first chapter I came upon a passage that served to completely shatter whatever vestiges of pride I had left.

*"Brothers, think of what you were when you were called. Not many of you were wise by human standards; not many were influential; not many were of noble birth. But God chose the foolish things of the world to shame the wise; God chose the weak things of the world to shame the strong. He chose the lowly things of this world and the despised things – and the things that are not – to nullify the things that are, so that no one may boast before him. It is because of him that you are in Christ Jesus, who has become for us wisdom from God – that is, our righteousness, holiness and redemption. Therefore, as it is written, 'Let him who boasts boast in the Lord.'"*

As I started to reflect on those verses, my phone rang. I glanced at the screen. It was Craig Diehl from the Observer.

"Evan? This is Craig."

"Hi, Craig."

"Listen, I'm sorry I was tied up earlier. "

"No problem. I understand this business."

"Yeah. Listen, Evan, I'll cut to the chase. I've decided to withdraw the job offer."

Sometimes words have a way of hanging in mid-air, then slowly floating to the floor before their meaning penetrates the psyche. This was such an occasion for me. Time seemed to stop. Finally I grasped what he had said. I gave no response. I had no idea how long it was before Craig spoke again.

"Evan? Are you there?"

"Yeah. Yeah, I'm here, Craig."

"I'm sorry, Evan. I really appreciate your being honest with me this afternoon, but I'm afraid we just can't take a chance. We want independent-minded reporters, but not free agents."

For a brief moment I regretted ever being truthful about my untruthfulness. My career aspirations were suddenly going up in smoke. But then somehow, miraculously, before I could even think to argue with him or beg for another chance, I became enveloped in a peace beyond comprehension. In some inexplicable way, I knew everything was going to be okay. His next words confirmed it.

"Besides, you found religion today. You probably won't be interested in being a reporter anymore." He could not stifle a chuckle.

Finally I was prepared to speak. "Actually, Craig, with all due respect, I think being a follower of Jesus Christ and being a newspaper reporter are not incompatible."

He seemed to catch himself, realizing his last statement may have been inappropriate. "Maybe so. You may yet have a long career in the newspaper business. I'm sorry it can't be with the Observer." I had the strange sense that my newfound faith was the real reason for his decision. Even so, I was determined not to challenge him.

"Well, I appreciate your call, Craig. Really, I do."

"Best of luck to you, Evan. Take care of yourself."

"You too."

With that, it was clear that my life had taken a radical turn and there was no turning back. I glanced down at the Bible, still open to 1 Corinthians. My eyes locked on to a verse in chapter 2: *"No eye has seen, no ear has heard, no mind has conceived what God has prepared for those who love him."*

Reading those words, I felt exhilarated. What kind of path had I set out on? Sam's caution about rough times was proving to be true. I just hadn't expected it to happen so soon. But I had no regrets.

# 9

I awoke the next morning without the assistance of the alarm clock. The night's sleep had not altered my mood. Even with the passage of time I still felt a never-before-experienced sense of serenity in the midst of such a major and unexpected turn in my life.

I was anxious to see if my op-ed was in the paper, so I jumped out of bed, opened the door and picked up the morning edition. Even though I had access to all the copies I could want at the office, I had subscribed to the Mirror since the day I was hired, feeling a sense of responsibility to contribute to the circulation rolls.

I grabbed the front section and quickly flipped to the editorial page. There was the op-ed! I read through it. True to his word, Dave had not changed a thing. I was anxious to get to the office so I could thank him in person. I got dressed, had a quick bowl of cereal, and drove over.

When I walked in, Dave was again talking to someone at his desk. I realized it was the same woman he had been speaking with the night before. He saw me and waved me in.

"Good morning, Evan. I'd like you to meet someone. Evan, meet Ann Walker."

I extended my hand. "Nice to meet you, Ann."

Dave smiled. "I've just hired Ann as your successor, Evan." I tried to hide the shock from my face. I thought it would take weeks before they found someone.

She smiled as well. "I hear I've got some big shoes to fill. By the way, congratulations on your new position."

"Uh…thanks." I knew she would find out soon enough, but wasn't ready to divulge my change of course just yet.

I looked over at Dave. "Dave, thanks for printing my op-ed. I really appreciate it."

"No problem, buddy. I always try to keep my word."

I decided to engage the new hire in conversation. "Congratulations, Ann. You couldn't have found a better editor than Dave. But watch out, he'll keep you on your toes."

Dave laughed. "Don't try to talk her out of it, Evan."

"Don't worry. So, Ann, I assume you've already got some newspaper experience under your belt. Otherwise Dave wouldn't have hired you."

"Yeah, I've been at my hometown paper for about a year and a half."

"Where's that?"

"Fairview."

*Fairview.* In a flash, I thought of the person living in Fairview whom I had assiduously avoided — my father. Suddenly the dark memories began to come over me like a wave. "Well, I'll let you two talk. Congratulations again, Ann. You're going to enjoy it here."

"Thank you, Evan."

I walked to my desk. I began to get an uneasy feeling in the pit of my stomach. Was I supposed to go visit my father? No. I couldn't. I wouldn't! It was too painful. Just the prospect of seeing that man's face made me feel ill. Still, I could not escape the mysterious sense that I was somehow being nudged in that direction. But what was the point? He would never listen to me.

Then I paused and reflected on the positive outcomes of the matters I had sensed I was supposed to do – the apology to Ralph, the confession to Dave, the op-ed…and, of course, even the phone call to Craig Diehl. On the surface, that one had turned out disastrously. But it had also been immensely gratifying, outward appearances notwithstanding. It stood to reason that I should submit to divine guidance in this case too.

I silently uttered a prayer. "I'll tell you what. If I find an address, I'll go. If I don't, I won't." I wasn't sure if it was appropriate to bargain with God, but felt it was a fair offer on my part.

I got online to see if I could find a listing. There was none. I felt a momentary sense of relief at being off the hook. But the feeling persisted. I remembered the story of Paul and Silas suffering in a putrid Roman jail. Who was I to pick and choose which directives I would follow and which I wouldn't? I knew it was time to take another drive.

\* \* \* \* \*

As I approached Fairview, I again started to wrestle with my feelings. Once again I broached the subject. "Are you sure about this, God? I don't know if I can face him after what he did."

I thought about the woman at the well in the Bible story. Jesus had forgiven her, and she in turn had forgiven any perceived slights toward the townspeople and told them what Jesus had done. I remembered the profound sense of guilt that had come over me the day before, followed by the liberation and jubilation I had experienced when I received the judge's forgiveness. "Okay, I'll do it. But please help me find him. I can't do this on my own."

As I drove into town, I realized it wouldn't be easy. Fairview was small, probably a third of the size of Franklin, with a population of around 20,000. But without an address, searching for him would be like looking for a needle in a haystack. I stopped at a convenience store and asked for their phone book. Maybe it was listed here but not online. There was a Jamieson, but no Jamison. How should I proceed? I again sought divine direction.

I glanced absent-mindedly down the street and prepared to return to my car when I did a double-take. There was a sign – "Roxy's Bar & Grill." Should I bother? It couldn't hurt.

When I walked inside, the smell of liquor was pronounced. My first instinct was to turn around and leave, but then remembered I was not on this quest for my own benefit.

I walked up to the bartender, who was wiping the counter.

"Excuse me. I'm looking for someone."

"You want a drink? It's Happy Hour – all drinks two for one."

No, thanks."

"You sure?" I shook my head.

He squirted some cleanser on the counter. "Okay, who you looking for?"

"A man named Nicholas Jamison. He's in his 50s."

"Nicholas Jamison. You mean Nick?"

"You know him?"

"You might say that." He grinned. "He's helped keep this place in business over the years."

Inwardly I marveled at the unseen hand that was guiding me. I looked around. There were three or four patrons. None of them looked familiar, though it had been so long that I probably wouldn't recognize him anyway.

"Is he here now?"

"No, lately he's only come in a couple of days a week."

"I don't suppose you know where he lives, do you?"

"I should. I've given him a ride home enough times. He only lives about a mile from here."

"Do you happen to know his address?"

He scratched his ear. "I know what road he lives on, but I can't remember the street number. I only know his house by sight. But it's easy. Just go south on Fairview Avenue about eight blocks and turn left on Barrington. Go about four blocks and turn right on Huffman. His house is a few doors down on the right. He's got an old green Chevy Impala with a few dents in it."

"Thanks a lot."

"Don't mention it."

As I opened the door to leave, I felt prompted to say something I had never before uttered to anyone: "God bless you!"

The bartender smiled and said, "Come on back for that drink later. And bring Nick!"

I got in my car and proceeded down Fairview Avenue. I spotted Barrington and made a left. My heart rate accelerated and my palms started getting clammy as I inched closer. I was about to do what I had once considered inconceivable – stand face to face with my father — and I was becoming filled with dread.

I saw the sign for Huffman and turned right. I slowed to look for the Impala. This appeared to be a rough neighborhood. Some of the houses had trash strewn about the yard. In someone's driveway was a car on blocks. One house had a window that looked like a rock had been thrown through it. I peered ahead. There in a driveway was the green Impala just as the bartender had described it — full of dents.

I parked and slowly emerged from the car. As I walked toward the front door, I had another flashback to my dream and the fear I had felt as I prepared to enter the first cell. That was how I felt now. The door was slightly ajar. I knocked a few times and braced myself. No response. I knocked again.

Apparently he was home since the car was in the driveway and the door wasn't closed all the way. Maybe he was asleep. I knocked harder, and this time the door popped open. I couldn't help but look inside. Someone had collapsed on the floor! Was it my father?

I rushed in and ran over to the man on the floor. This had to be my dad. Who else could it be? Had he had a heart attack? Was he alive? I noticed his chest move up and down. I breathed a sigh of relief. Then I saw it — an empty whiskey bottle on the floor. The man was stone drunk.

\* \* \* \* \*

I decided to try waking him, but opted not to call him "Dad" until he sobered up, as the shock might be too great for him. I chose instead to call him by name. "Nick? Mr. Jamison? Are you okay? Can you wake up?" He didn't budge.

It had been 16 years and nothing had changed. He was still just a no-good drunk. I was repulsed. Here, sprawled on the floor, was the man who had left my mother to shoulder everything as a single parent, and had walked away from me, his only child. I was tempted to strike him in the face — not once or twice, but over and over. He deserved no less. For a moment I even entertained the thought of putting a pillow over his face and putting him out of my misery. No one would ever know.

But just as quickly I remembered that someone, in fact, would know, and that someone had led me here for a purpose. I could not and would not lay a finger on him. But why had God led me here to witness this? Hadn't I already been through enough in the 24 hours since I had become one of his followers? I had sacrificed my career! What more did he want from me? Without warning the tears returned. I collapsed on the liquor-stained couch.

I cried out. "Why did you bring me here — to see this? I'm not strong enough! It hurts too much! Please let me leave and never come back. I just can't handle it." I cried until I was emptied of tears. I dabbed my eyes and looked down. My father hadn't moved an inch in spite of my outburst. I had seen enough. I got up and walked out to the car. My relationship with God had gotten off to a rousing start, but now doubts were taking the upper hand.

I started the engine and prepared to put it in reverse when I happened to glance down at the passenger seat and saw the Bible Sam had given me. Next to it was my reporter's notebook with the verses I had jotted down. I grasped the gear shift and looked over my shoulder to back out, then took one more glimpse at the notebook – *Isaiah ch. 53, 700 years before birth; Isaiah 7, Zech. 9, Psalm 22.*

I took a breath and decided to put off my departure long enough to read one of those chapters. I selected Psalm 22. I turned to the table of contents and found where the Psalms were located, then tracked down #22. I began to read and could not believe my eyes.

*"My God, my God, why have you forsaken me? Why are you so far from saving me, so far from the words of my groaning? O my God, I cry out by day, but you do not answer, by night, and am not silent."*

That was exactly how I felt! But how could one of the Bible writers say something like that? Wasn't there some kind of rule prohibiting that kind of thing? On I read.

*"Yet you are enthroned as the Holy One. You are the praise of Israel. In you our fathers put their trust; they trusted and you delivered them. They cried to you and were saved; in you they trusted and were not disappointed."*

The words "trust" and "trusted" jumped out from the page at me. In the midst of my meltdown on my father's couch, two words had kept floating around quietly in my head, words I had tried to ignore: *"Trust me. Trust me."*

I resumed my reading. *"But I am a worm and not a man, scorned by men and despised by the people. All who see me mock me; they hurl insults, shaking their heads. 'He trusts in the LORD; let the LORD rescue him. Let him deliver him, since he delights in him.'"*

Were all the psalms like this? With my car's engine still running, I continued.

*"Yet you brought me out of the womb; you made me trust in you even at my mother's breast. From birth I was cast upon you; from my mother's womb you have been my God. Do not be far from me, for trouble is near and there is no one to help. Many bulls surround me; strong bulls of Bashan encircle me. Roaring lions tearing their prey open their mouths wide against me. I am poured out like water, and all my bones are out of joint. My heart has turned to wax; it has melted away within me. My strength is dried up like a potsherd, and my tongue sticks to the roof of my mouth; you lay me in the dust of death. Dogs have surrounded me; a band of evil men has encircled me; they have pierced my hands and my feet. I can count all my bones. People stare and gloat over me. They divide my garments among them and cast lots for my clothing."*

While I did not have a strong familiarity with the crucifixion, that gruesome event was obviously what these verses were describing. The message was clear. I turned off the engine and took a moment to again ask forgiveness for my wavering trust and my vengeful thoughts. I got out of the car, Bible in hand, and went back inside.

\* \* \* \* \*

I peeked in the door to see if my father had awakened. He still had not moved from his previous spot. Not knowing how long it would take for him to sober up, I decided to contact Dave. I had a week of unused vacation for which the Mirror was going to reimburse me, so I asked Dave if I could go ahead and use it this week. He granted my request, which soothed my conscience. I had begun feeling uneasy about being paid for my regular duties since I had wound up spending so much time on personal matters this week.

With that out of the way, all I had to do now was wait. I decided to resume my Bible reading, so I finished Psalm 22, then re-read the astonishing chapter 53 of Isaiah. After that I turned back to Isaiah 7 and found the prophecy about the virgin birth, then went back to Sam's favorite, the Gospel of John, and resumed where I had left off last night with chapter 5.

> *"Some time later, Jesus went up to Jerusalem for a feast of the Jews. Now there is in Jerusalem near the Sheep Gate a pool, which in Aramaic is called Bethesda and which is surrounded by five covered colonnades. Here a great number of disabled people used to lie — the blind, the lame, the paralyzed. One who was there had been an invalid for thirty-eight years. When Jesus saw him lying there and learned that he had been in this condition for a long time, he asked him, 'Do you want to get well?' 'Sir,' the invalid replied, 'I have no one to help me into the pool when the water is stirred. While I am trying to get in, someone else goes down ahead of me.' Then Jesus said to him, 'Get up! Pick up your mat and walk.' At once the man was cured; he picked up his mat and walked."*

Reading that story made me all the more eager to learn more about this extraordinary Savior. In him was the compassion, the empathy, that I had always lacked. It also served to remind me that he was the one who had the power to change my father. Indeed, I was powerless to alter the course of my father's life, just as I couldn't change the world as a journalist. I read the story again and was struck by the depth of Jesus' seemingly simple question: *"Do you want to get well?"* At first blush one would assume the man would say yes, but in fact he could have just as easily said no if he were comfortable having other people take care of his needs. Fortunately the man had the wisdom to say yes. But would my father?

By this time it was late in the afternoon and I was getting drowsy. A short nap would do me a world of good. I went and looked for his bedroom, then thought better of it. I didn't want him waking up and finding someone he didn't know sleeping on his bed. Better to stay on the smelly couch so I could hear him.

When I awoke, the sun had set and the room was dark. How long had I been asleep? I checked my watch. It was 8:30. It had been at least two hours. A light was on in a nearby room. I looked down and saw my father's shadowy figure on the floor. Incredibly, he had barely moved in all that time. I carefully stepped over him to follow the light and discovered it was the kitchen.

Dirty dishes were piled high. How could anyone live like this? I walked over and started washing the dishes with the small amount of soap he had. I also used the occasion to pray for my father. The combination of those tasks – the lengthy dishwashing and the prayer, in addition to the Bible verses I had read earlier – had a transformative effect on me. I found myself carried beyond just a grudging willingness to talk to my father to an earnest desire for him to experience what I had experienced.

I heard a sound behind me and turned around. There stood my father — unshaven, wobbly, glassy-eyed — with a baseball bat held aloft in his hands.

"Don't move or I'll bring this down right on your head! What are you doing in my house?"

"Don't worry! It's okay. I'm just doing the dishes."

"Why? Who are you?"

I hesitated, not sure how he would respond to a truthful answer, especially with that weapon in his hand.

"I said who are you? And what are you doing here?"

"I'm your son — Evan."

With that, the bat slipped out of his hands and fell to the floor.

# 10

I knew so little about the man standing before me. Over the years I had coaxed a few kernels out of Mom. She shared how he was highly intelligent but not very ambitious. He had held a series of mid-level jobs in the state government but never managed to advance very far.

She had never met his mother, who had died of ovarian cancer just before his sophomore year in high school. His father, my grandfather, whom I didn't remember because he had died of a heart attack when I was only three, was, according to my mother, a critical father for whom nothing my dad did was ever good enough. One time, in a rare moment of candor, Mom had expressed the opinion that his father's death, rather than giving Dad a sense of release, had actually somehow contributed to his downward spiral.

Dad stumbled to the lone chair at the kitchen table and put his hand to his head. He winced…obviously suffering the effects of his latest binge. Now that I had divulged my identity, I hoped to receive a warm greeting. Sadly, he seemed incapable of that.

"How did you find me here?" he groused.

Well, Mom told me years ago that you had moved to Fairview."

"Yeah, but my address is unlisted."

"Oh, the bartender at Roxy's Bar & Grill told me where you live."

"Manny. He'll be hearing from me about this. How did you end up there, anyway? Forget it. It doesn't matter. Well, I don't have any money, if that's what you're here for. I'm renting this house and I don't own anything of value."

"I'm not here for money."

"Did your mother send you to track me down?"

"No! I found you myself. She doesn't even know I'm here."

"Then why did you come?" He still sounded suspicious.

I hadn't intended on broaching the subject of my newfound faith so early in our conversation, but I was so taken aback by his hostility that I decided to proceed with it immediately. "Well, do you want the truth?"

"Yeah."

"Okay, the truth is that I've hated you for a long time. The truth is that I stayed as far away from Fairview as I could since the day I heard that you moved here. The truth is that even today I tried to talk myself out of coming. The truth is that I almost turned around and left when I saw you passed out on the floor. But the truth also is that someone very important wanted me to see you."

"I thought you said your mother doesn't know you're here."

"I'm not referring to Mom."

"Then who?"

"Your creator."

"What are you talking about?"

"I'm talking about God, Dad."

He rolled his eyes in disgust. "There is no God. Or if there is, he's a petty tyrant who spends all his free time making sure people like me never catch a break."

It was obvious that this man had not changed at all. Everything about him conformed with my distant childhood memories. I still was torn between revulsion, on the one hand, and compassion, even hope, on the other. I sent up a quick silent prayer appealing for help, and the compassionate side again took the upper hand. My expression and tone softened as I began my response.

"I actually was an agnostic for as long as I can remember. The only thing I truly believed in was myself. I was convinced that if there was a higher power, it must be an impersonal force, because I couldn't deal with the thought that there was a God with an actual personality." I looked at the angry man slouched in the chair in front of me and felt overwhelmed with pity, yet was determined not to waffle on delivering the cold, hard truth. "I'm not saying this to be spiteful, Dad, but I thought if there really was a personal God, he was probably like you, and I just couldn't handle that. So I reached the safer conclusion that the deity must be impersonal and unknowable. But just yesterday I made a great discovery – that God is not only knowable, but he wants to be known, and he made that possible through Jesus Christ."

He made no reply, but the softening of my tone seemed to ease the tension in the air. I was eager to elaborate on yesterday's dramatic events, but conversely I had no desire to overload him in his present condition. Since he was giving me no indication he wanted me to leave, I figured I would have time to raise the subject in more detail later. For now, I just wanted to get acquainted.

"I'm glad to see you, Dad. I'm not going to lie and tell you you look good, but just the same, I'm glad I came." I noticed the corners of his mouth turn up just a little, though the dominant expression on his face suggested he was developing a wicked hangover.

"So are you working, Dad?" Inwardly I thought it a silly question; I could not imagine him being able to hold a job.

He slowly shifted in his chair. "Yeah, some." He put his hands to his head and rubbed his temples.

"That's good. What kind of work are you doing?"

"This and that."

At the risk of sounding nosy, I dug deeper. "Oh, like what?"

"I took early retirement from the government, so I do odd jobs here and there to keep myself busy."

To keep himself busy? Who was he kidding? Early retirement meant a much smaller pension. He probably had to work to cover his rent…in addition to his frequent trips to the liquor store.

"Was there a reason you retired early?"

"Yeah. I grew tired of their treatment. They were imbeciles. I couldn't take it anymore."

I didn't want to hear it, so I changed the subject. "Are you hungry, Dad? I am. I took a nap and slept right through dinner."

"Help yourself to what's in the fridge."

I opened the refrigerator door. Ketchup, mustard, and stale-looking bologna were its only contents.

"You can check the pantry too."

I looked and saw a jar of nuts. I opened it and bit into one. It had to be months old, if not older.

"You're not eating much these days, are you, Dad?"

"No. Haven't had much of an appetite lately."

I felt sick to think of what this man had done to himself. Then I remembered the account of Jesus and the man at the pool and Jesus' question: *"Do you want to get well?"* I wanted to run out and get him some nutritious foods…or any food, for that matter. No, I couldn't do that. If I went to the store, he might take off for Roxy's. I settled for ordering a pizza. I'd be sure to get it loaded with vegetables for Dad's sake.

"Have you got a phone book, Dad?"

"In the drawer. Why?"

"I want to order some pizza."

"Pizza? No, what say we go to Roxy's? Manny makes a good Reuben."

What kind of fool did he take me for? "No, if it's all right with you, I'd rather eat here. I don't feel like going out."

"Suit yourself."

After ordering the pizza, I suggested we go sit on the couch. He was still unsteady but managed to make his way into the other room. He grabbed the remote and turned on the TV.

"Is it all right if we leave the TV off for a while, Dad?"

"Why?"

"I figured we could talk."

He frowned. "Not about your mother."

"Okay, not about Mom." With that, he grudgingly clicked off the television.

\* \* \* \*

I wasn't sure how to proceed with the conversation. Then, to my surprise, he took the initiative. "I still can't believe you came here to see me...but you're looking good, Evan."

"Thanks."

"How old are you now?"

"Twenty-six."

"Is that right? What kind of work do you do?"

"I'm a newspaper reporter."

"Is that so? Which paper?

"I've been at the Franklin Mirror for a couple of years. I just got hired by the Capital Observer, but" —

"The Observer?"

"Yes, but" —

"From what I recall, that's the best paper in the state."

"Yes, it is, but" —

"I suppose congratulations are in order. You've obviously done quite well for yourself."

I knew such a compliment must have been difficult for him, which made me appreciate it all the more. "Thank you, Dad. But actually, as of this moment I'm unemployed. They withdrew their offer."

"Why did they do that?"

"Ostensibly because I added a little extra seasoning to one of my stories, which I shouldn't have done. But I suspect that's not the real reason, or at least not the only reason."

"Oh, I know what it is. You're your father's own son, that's what it is! I always got the raw end of the deal, and now it's happening to you. Like father, like son."

"Actually, Dad, I think the man who hired me was uneasy with my newfound faith."

"Then you should sue for religious discrimination! I don't agree with all that Bible mumbo jumbo, but it's illegal to fire someone based on religion. You need to get a good lawyer."

"No, Dad. It's okay, really. For one thing, I'm not going to raise a stink over something for which I have no tangible proof. But more importantly, I'm at peace with it. Believe me, when he first told me, I was devastated. I was crushed."

"I know the feeling!"

"Well, but very quickly I was reminded that my life is now in God's hands and everything is going to be all right."

"Well, you can say that now. You're young. Just wait till they've stepped on you for 20 years!"

He kept fishing for the opportunity to spill his tale of woe, but I wasn't biting. "Dad, my faith may be new, but I know it's real. Until two days ago, I thought the world was my oyster. But lurking just underneath the surface was a gnawing desperation within me. When it bubbled to the surface, it seemed like it would destroy me. Instead I have discovered a new life that gives me something I never even imagined."

"Oh? What's that?"

"Peace. Contentment. Joy."

He scowled. "If there's really a God out there, why did he take your grandmother?"

"Grandma Alice?"

"Yes. He took her from me. That was the turning point, when my life started to go downhill. I was only 15 – too young to lose my mother! And she was one of his most devoted followers. Explain that one to me – how a kind Christian woman could be taken by cancer and get outlived for years by a cold-hearted man who cared not a whit about religion."

\* \* \* \* \*

Just then there was a knock at the door. The pizza had arrived. I opened the box, took out a slice, put it on a plate and offered it to my father. It looked delicious. He shook his head. "No, thanks. I'm not really hungry."

I found his response rather odd, but the growl of my stomach and the sight of the pizza were too overwhelming to allow me to give that more than a passing thought. I grabbed a slice and bit into it. Mouth-watering. Fairview was not without its virtues.

As I took a second bite, it dawned on me that it would be appropriate to give thanks to God for the food. Although my dad wasn't joining me in eating, I said a simple prayer aloud.

Four slices later, my appetite sated, I sat contentedly on the couch, blissfully unaware of the bombshell my father was about to deliver.

"Evan?"

"Finally ready for some pizza?"

"I'm dying."

What? Surely I misunderstood. He was only 54. "What did you say?"

"I said I'm dying, simple as that."

"Do you have cancer?"

"No — cirrhosis."

Of course! That explained his total lack of interest in food. He was literally drinking himself to death.

"Couldn't you go to detox or something?"

"No, it's too late for that. My liver is pretty much shot." He looked off into space.

I wasn't sure how to handle such jolting news. I had heeded the call to finally visit the man who had abandoned me, only to learn that his days were numbered.

"Evan, can we talk about this tomorrow? It's getting late. I need to go to bed." I looked at my watch. It was close to 11:00. "I've got a second bedroom, but there's no bed in it. You're free to sleep on the couch if you'd like. You can check the closet…I might even have a sheet and blanket."

It took only a moment to decide to accept his offer. I couldn't stop him from drinking, but perhaps my presence would provide at least a measure of deterrence.

\* \* \* \* \*

I awoke with a start. It was still dark. Where was I? Oh, yes, in my father's house. I pushed the light button on my watch. It was 5:45. Since I was wide awake, it occurred to me this would be a good time to continue my reading of the Bible. I decided to re-read the account of Jesus' healing of the paralytic in John 5, then continued on, highlighted by his powerful rebuke of the religious leaders in chapter 8, the extraordinary story of the raising of Lazarus in chapter 11, then on to a great promise in John 14 – *"In my Father's house are many rooms."* I was beginning to understand how Sam had become so attached to this book.

After concluding my reading, I peeked in Dad's room to find him still sleeping soundly. I dashed out to buy a drive-thru breakfast and stopped at a store to pick up some cleaning supplies. Upon my return, I checked on him to find him still asleep. I then went to work scrubbing the bathroom and the kitchen floor, followed by a good dusting of the living room area.

Finally I decided it was time for a break, so I plopped down on the couch and turned on the news. Just then Dad walked in. I smiled broadly. "Good morning!"

He frowned, then scrunched his nose. "What's that smell?"

"Disinfectant. I gave the house a good cleaning. Your bedroom is next."

"You really don't need to do that."

"I know. But I want to." It was true. I was finding satisfaction in giving his house a good cleaning. He may have destroyed his life, but that didn't mean I couldn't at least try to make things a bit more bearable for him.

He sat down on the couch and joined me in watching the news. After a weather update, they showed a report of a Marine who had come home from deployment overseas and surprised his daughter by showing up at her school unannounced. The camera showed a close-up of the little girl looking up lovingly at her father, transfixed on him, even in awe of him. The irony did not escape me. Here I sat next to the man who had chosen a bottle over me.

I muted the sound on the TV. "Dad?"

"Yeah."

"Did you notice that story about the Marine and his daughter?"

"Yeah."

"I want you to know it hurt not having you ever come home to me like that soldier came home to his daughter." I paused. "But I also want you to know I forgive you and I love you."

He remained silent.

"I also want you to know that I don't have an answer to what you asked me last night. Dad, I don't know why your mom died and your dad lived on. This whole faith thing is new to me. But to be honest, I don't think I ever could have given you a satisfactory answer to that, even if I had been a Christian for years. But one thing I've learned in a very short time is that God is not like an earthly father, and that includes your own father. Nothing you did was good enough for your father. You couldn't live up to his standards. Well, no one lives up to God's standards, but the difference is he's willing to forgive and restore. God can be trusted. He is the perfect Father. He proved it by giving his own son to die for our sins."

I turned and glanced at him. I was surprised to see his eyes misting ever so slightly.

"Dad, I've started reading the Bible. I read an amazing story about Jesus walking up to a crippled man and asking a simple question: *"Do you want to get well?"* Dad, in a way you're like that crippled man. In fact, we're all like him. We're all in need. The question is, do *you* want to get well?"

He started to shake his head. "I already told you it's too late for me. I'm dying."

"Maybe it is too late for you physically. But it's not too late spiritually until you take your last breath."

He sat in silence and seemed unprepared to respond. I had no idea what was going through his mind. I concluded it was time to give him some space. Understanding I couldn't stay by his side 24 hours a day, I got up, stripped the sheets off his bed, grabbed a mountain of dirty clothes reeking of alcohol, and ventured out to look for a laundromat. I was certain I would return to find him once again in a stupor, but was willing to take baby steps in this process. I hoped he was as well.

*Death Row Journal*

\* \* \* \* \*

As I watched the clothes go through the rinse cycle, I took stock of my trip to Fairview. I considered the facts at hand. My father was dying and only gradually warming to my re-emergence in his life. I had no job. My lease was expiring in three days. Yet in spite of these dire circumstances, I was filled with hope.

That reflection prompted me to reach into my back pocket for the Bible. Not there. I must have left it at the house. So instead I took the opportunity to pray. I prayed for my father. I prayed for my mother. I prayed for Sam. I prayed for the kids I had tutored. After putting the clothes in the dryer, I prayed about my own situation, asking for guidance in regard to a job and a place to live. I wrapped up by expressing my gratitude for my ever-growing awareness of God's presence and my newfound joy. With that, I folded the clothes and headed back to my dad's.

As I lugged the clothes basket through the door, my father was nowhere to be seen. My heart sank. I feared what that might mean. His car was in the driveway, so he had to be here somewhere. I peeked in his room to observe that he was not in his bed either. Just as I was about to look elsewhere, I happened to notice his bathroom door was closed. That explained it. Obviously I should have given him the benefit of the doubt. Then again, maybe he was imbibing in the only place he could escape my watchful eye.

I put the clothes away and walked into the kitchen to get a cup of water. There on the table was my Bible. To my great surprise, it was open. I was sure I had not left it that way. Next to it was my reporter's notebook with the Bible verses I had scribbled down earlier. I looked at the Bible. It was turned to Isaiah 53.

Just then I noticed movement out of the corner of my eye. I looked up. There again stood my father in the door, in the very spot I had first caught sight of him the day before. Gone altogether was the anger...replaced, judging by his expression, with despair.

"Are you okay, Dad?"

He remained in the doorway. "I took the liberty of borrowing your Bible." His lip was quivering slightly. "I also looked at your notebook. I hope you don't mind."

"Not at all."

I was unsure what to say or do next. We both stood in silence for several moments. Finally he slowly began to speak, all the while looking toward the floor. "I...I was reading... Isaiah. I remembered it from my youth. My mother...used to read that to me." He looked up at me and his eyes were beginning to fill with tears.

Suddenly he collapsed to his knees. Had he been drinking again? He began to wail. I could not understand what he was saying. The only words I could decipher were "I'm sorry" repeated over and over in the midst of his lament.

Although I suspected his outburst was caused by alcohol, I could not help but run over and kneel down next to him and try to comfort him. "It's okay, Dad. I'm here. I love you."

Finally I was able to discern more of what he was saying. "I killed him! I killed him!"

"Dad...Dad! I'm here. What are you trying to say?"

"My mother...when she was dying, she told me what she had told me a thousand times before...that God loved me and demonstrated it by allowing his son to die for me. But I blamed him for letting her die. I turned my back and walked away from him. Now look at me! I deserted my wife and son and I'm drinking myself to death. It's *my* sins that killed him!" His tears intensified. "And now...you're back in my life...helping me. Why? Why!?"

I leaned over him and put my arm around him. "Dad, I told you why. God wanted me to come so I could tell you — and show you — that he loves you."

"How could he love me? I put Christ on the cross. It says it in black and white. I killed him!"

"We all did! Your sins did, but mine did too. It says, 'We *all* have gone astray.' Did you read the whole chapter?"

"I don't need to."

"Oh, I think you do." I got up, grabbed the Bible off the table and returned to the floor. By this time he had sat up and was wiping his eyes.

"Listen to this." I quickly skimmed it and found an appropriate place to start. "*Yet it was the LORD's will to crush him and cause him to suffer, and though the LORD makes his life a guilt offering, he will see his offspring and prolong his days, and the will of the LORD will prosper in his hand. After the suffering of his soul, he will see the light of life and be satisfied; by his knowledge my righteous servant will justify many, and he will bear their iniquities.*"

I waited for his eyes to meet mine. "Dad, this says it was God's will for him to die so we could be justified. I don't know much about theology, but I know 'justify' is a legal term and it means our guilt is taken away. This also says God brought him back to life and he's alive today. I know that for a fact!"

He shook his head. "How could he love me? I don't deserve it!"

"Do you think I do? I was full of pride and arrogance and hate."

"At least you didn't drink yourself to death."

All of a sudden it dawned on me that he had not, in fact, been drinking. There was no hint of alcohol on his breath and he was speaking clearly. What had seared his conscience was not a drink but a Bible passage written thousands of years ago.

"Dad, I don't think God makes a distinction between sins. Believe me, I thought I was on a different plane than you because I didn't drink. But God didn't love me because

I chose to refrain from drinking. He didn't love me because I was some virtuous person. In fact, he loved me not because I was good but in spite of the fact that I was bad. I didn't earn his love. No one can. That's why it's called grace."

"I still feel like what I've done is worse."

"Well, even if it were, that doesn't mean it's unforgivable. And he wants to forgive you! Do you remember what I quoted you earlier that Jesus said to the paralyzed man? *"Do you want to get well?"* That's what he's asking you, Dad. Do you want to get well? Do you want to be made whole?"

"It's hard to believe. I've hated myself for a long time, son, and now you're telling me that God loves me."

"I hated you too, Dad. But God never stopped loving you. He's always wanted to adopt you as his child, but it has to be on his terms, not yours. It's not about you. It's about him and what he did for you on the cross."

He sat quietly, deep in thought, so I took the opportunity to pray. After a few minutes I broke the silence. "You know, Dad, everything in our nature tells us to pursue our own self-interest. Our culture reflects that. We are bombarded with messages that we deserve the best job, the best car, the best life. But that's a lie. I was completely absorbed with my own ambition, yet I was also completely miserable. I didn't start living until I received Christ's forgiveness and handed the reins of my life to him."

A passage that I had read from the Gospel of John came to mind. I flipped back to the first chapter and started skimming through. Found it! Chapter 1, starting with verse 10. "Listen to this, Dad. *'He was in the world, and though the world was made through him, the world did not recognize him. He came to that which was his own, but his own did not receive him. Yet to all who received him, to those who believed in his name, he gave the right to become children of God – children born not of natural descent, nor of human decision or a husband's will, but born of God.'"*

I repeated one part for emphasis. *"'Yet to all who received him, to those who believed in his name, he gave the right to become children of God.'* Remember what I said, Dad. He's not like the man you grew up with. He's the perfect father, and he wants you to be his child."

With that, his tears returned. He fell once again to his knees, put his face to the freshly scrubbed linoleum, and began to cry out. "Lord, please forgive me! I'm sorry for rejecting you all these years. I'm sorry for all the things I've done. I want to be your child if you'll take me."

I could scarcely believe what I was witnessing. The joy I had experienced in the parking lot of City Hall was now matched, if not exceeded, which I had not thought possible.

When his prayer was done and his tears had subsided, I helped him to his feet and embraced him. Was this really happening? I was completely reconciled to the man I had hated all my life. In fact, now we were more than father and son. We were *brothers*.

\* \* \* \* \*

As I drove onto Fairview Avenue to pick up some groceries, an idea popped into my head. What was there to stop me from moving to Fairview and helping my father get through his final days? Indeed, what was there to stop me from taking up residence in his second bedroom — contingent, of course, on his agreement with such a plan?

I then remembered the woman who had filled my position at the *Mirror*. Her last job had been in Fairview, and it probably needed filling. Would I be willing to lower myself by taking a step decidedly down the career ladder, at less pay? It took but a moment to answer: Of course! I enjoyed a good laugh at my own expense.

I looked up the address for the *Fairview Star*. When I walked into the tiny office, the editor/columnist, Edna

Dowdy, was harried, trying to handle all the duties herself, but welcomed me in to talk. I inquired about the job. When I described my work experience, she was skeptical of my interest. But in keeping with my new policy of candor, I laid it on the line and told her what had happened with the Observer.

She became convinced I would be a fitting successor to her recently departed reporter. In fact, she said she too was a believer and invited me to her church. "No pressure...but I'll give you all the tough assignments if you decide to attend another church." She winked good-naturedly. "Seriously, I think you'd like it. I love it there. I'm involved in the children's ministry."

By the time I turned onto my father's street, it was late afternoon. I had to approach with care because the road was teeming with kids. When I walked in the door, Dad was sitting on the couch, reading the Bible. "Guess what, Dad – I got a job."

"What – while you were out?"

"Yep."

"Where?"

"The Fairview Star. I'll be their lead columnist."

"You're kidding!" He smiled broadly.

"Well, I needed a job, and I happened to know they had an opening." I sat down next to him. "Dad, I've been thinking. I need a place to stay and you need help with the rent. If it's okay with you, I'd like to move into your spare bedroom."

"You want to live here, in this house?" I started to brace myself. Would he rebuff my proposal? "I'd love it!"

As I put away the groceries, I was ecstatic. But then came the somber realization that what lay ahead would not be a walk in the park. It would be tough sledding to watch my father's physical condition deteriorate. I also knew that he still might face strong temptation in regard to alcohol. Even so, my confidence remained unflinching that I was precisely where I was supposed to be.

That night my father managed to keep down some soup and green beans without getting ill. By far the best aspect of the meal was the simple yet previously unimaginable act of a father and son breaking bread together and enjoying one another's company. It truly was a miracle.

After another night on the couch, the next morning I walked out to my car for the return trip to Franklin to pack up my things. A boy of about 10 approached me on his way to school. "Hey, mister, you know the guy who lives here?"

I looked down and smiled. "I sure do. He's my father. And I'm going to be your new neighbor. I'll be moving in here!"

"That's cool. Hey, do you have any candy?"

"Afraid not."

As I settled into the driver's seat, I had an epiphany. These kids needed guidance. They needed structure. They needed tutoring. They needed the Lord. Here on this street was a second chance to work with troubled kids, only this time with the proper motivation and the divine empowerment to do it right. Maybe Edna, my new boss, could send over some children's workers from her church to help.

\* \* \* \* \*

As I drove the winding road back to Franklin, I shook my head at the wonder of all that had transpired in the course of a few days. When I reached my apartment, I grabbed my phone. I had an important call to make.

"Sam? This is Evan Jamison."

"Evan! I've been praying for you. How's everything going? Can we get together before you move? I'd love to see you."

I laughed. "That'd be great. But how much time do you have? I've got a lot to tell you!"